THE DISTANT PROMISE
GRAHAM'S RESOLUTION
BOOK 10

A. R. SHAW

Copyright © 2025 by A. R. Shaw

All rights reserved.

No part of this book may be reproduced in any form or by any electronic or mechanical means, including information storage and retrieval systems, without written permission from the author, except for the use of brief quotations in a book review.

For those who have carried burdens too heavy to bear, yet walk forward still. And for the distant promise of peace, love, and a future worth fighting for.

For Adam—my constant, my reason, my unbroken bond. And for those who hold onto hope, even when the world tells them to let go.

For Dennis…don't read this one :-)

Hope is the thing with feathers that perches in the soul —and sings the tune without the words, and never stops at all.

EMILY DICKINSON

CHAPTER 1- THE ROAD LEFT BEHIND

Graham lay in the darkness, his eyes tracing the faint lines of the tent's ceiling. The air was still, broken only by the sound of Paige's soft breathing beside him. She was curled on her side, her wild blond hair strewn across her face like a halo of pale gold. Though he had to admit, she was no angel—perhaps a fallen angel—but she was his angel whether she liked it or not, especially now. His hand rested on her belly, fingers splayed gently over the slight swell that held their future—three months along, by Clarisse's estimation. The life growing there was still fragile, a tiny, unexpected flame in the darkness of their world.

He was careful not to disturb her sleep, knowing how rare it was for her to rest deeply these days. Morning sickness had plagued her relentlessly, sapping her strength and leaving her thin and pale and grouchier than ever. But the nettle tea Elara had made—rich in magnesium and herbs—had helped. For the past few days, Paige had managed to keep food down, and that was at least something.

Graham's thumb brushed lightly over the hem of her shirt. The baby was so small he couldn't feel any movement yet, but he liked to think that somehow, some way, the child within knew he was there. That they were in this together, the three of them.

"Hold on," he whispered, barely more than a breath. "Just hold on."

He shifted slightly, brushing her tangled hair out of her face with a tenderness that felt foreign, almost fragile, in his rough hands. Paige murmured something in her sleep, her brow creasing as if she sensed his thoughts and his worries. He leaned in, pressing a gentle kiss to her temple.

Then, carefully, he slipped out of the bed, his movements slow and deliberate. The air outside the covers was cool against his skin, and he shivered as he pulled on his shirt, his gaze lingering on Paige's sleeping form. She looked so peaceful like this—at rest, her features softened, free from the constant fear and pain that marked their waking hours.

For a moment, he hesitated, his hand still resting on the tent flap. The urge to stay, to climb back into the warmth of the blankets and wrap himself around her, was strong. But he couldn't. Not now. There was too much to think about, too many decisions that needed to be made in the long term in their child was to survive.

With a quiet sigh, Graham stepped outside, the predawn light painting the camp in shades of blue and gray. The air was cold, crisp, and he breathed it in deeply, letting it clear the fog of sleep from his mind. He glanced back at the tent, where Paige slept on, oblivious to the world outside.

They deserved better than this—better than a life spent fighting, hiding, barely surviving.

Graham turned his gaze back to the dark outline of trees that marked the edge of the camp's perimeter. His eyes burned from lack of sleep, and every muscle in his body felt strung tight, like a wire stretched too far. He could still see Lawoaka's face every time he closed his eyes—bruised, dirty, desperate. She'd looked at him with a pleading gaze that cut through him like a knife.

"I'll come back," he'd promised. But with each day that passed, that promise felt more like a lie.

He'd made promises. But promises were easy to make and harder to keep.

"What would you have done, Rick?" he muttered into the stillness, his voice swallowed by the early morning silence.

Rick's voice echoed in his mind, faint but laced with that familiar humor. "What, you think I'd have some brilliant plan to sneak onto an island guarded by a hundred terrorists? Yeah, right."

Graham shook his head, a hollow chuckle escaping him. Rick would have been there to challenge him, push him, and keep him grounded. He missed that—missed his friend's steady presence like a part of himself had been torn away. It had only been a week since they'd buried Rick, and the wound was still open, fleshy, and raw.

Without thinking, Graham's feet carried him to the small clearing on the edge of the camp where they'd buried Rick right next to his old friend Steve. The one, long ago, who took the bullet meant for McCann. The dirt was still fresh, the cross they'd placed at the head of the grave a rough piece of wood with Rick's name burned into it. It wasn't much, but it was all they had.

Graham knelt beside the grave. Fresh wild daisies lay on the loose soil—Olivia or Bethany's doing, likely. The thought of Rick's widow, always tending to the needs of others while keeping her grief locked inside, made his throat tighten. "I don't know what to do, Rick. I can't see a way forward. Lawoaka... the others... I promised I'd come back for them, but I don't even know where to start. And everyone here, they miss you, man."

The wind answered back, stirred the trees overhead, the leaves rustling softly. He closed his eyes, letting the sounds wash over him, wishing more than anything that he could hear Rick's voice again—really hear it, not just the echoes in his head. But there was only silence.

"I'm not cut out for this," he whispered, his voice rough. "I don't know if I can do this alone. And my god, you would give me a hard time about Paige being pregnant. I would never hear the end of this."

A long moment passed before he finally stood, staring down at the grave for a beat longer. Then, he turned and made his way back to the camp, his steps heavy and slow.

The camp was beginning to stir when Graham reached the clinic. He waved as a tired Mark walked in off watch, knowing Marcy had just replaced him. He sensed trouble between the two but wasn't sure what it was, and he didn't have the time to figure it out either.

He pushed open the door flap, the scent of antiseptic and herbs filling his nose. Clarisse looked up from where she was standing beside the bed, her expression tight with worry.

"She's in and out," she said quietly, gesturing to the unconscious girl on the bed. "But she's stable. As stable as she can be, anyway."

Graham nodded, his gaze drifting over the girl's battered form. Her face was swollen beyond recognition, her eyes shut tight. Her arm was splinted, and bandages wrapped around her chest, hiding the broken ribs. Every inch of her seemed to scream with pain. And he had done nothing but watch.

"I think she's younger than we thought," Clarisse murmured, almost to herself. "I mean, I think she is. It's hard to tell with the swelling and the bruises, but... she can't be more than sixteen or seventeen."

Graham's chest tightened. "Are you kidding me? She's just a kid?" A kid who'd been through hell and back. And now she was here, in their care, and he had no idea how to help her. "Has she said anything?"

Clarisse shook her head. "No. Not a word. Arabic or otherwise. She's got to be terrified. We don't look like her people. She has no idea where she is or who she's with. So, I asked Sam to bring her clothes to Olivia since she's washing today. That at least her personal items would be familiar to her. But the thing is, Sam didn't bring them to her. Instead, he tossed them on the burn pile out back."

Graham frowned. "He burned her clothes. Why?"

Clarisse's gaze shifted, discomfort flickering across her face. "Because they were covered in blood. And…" She hesitated. "Because of what they represent. Sam said they were a symbol of… submission. He didn't want her wearing them again. He didn't want them in camp."

Graham let out a slow breath, glancing down at the girl. "And you?"

"I mean, I understand. But I think she should decide that for herself," Clarisse said softly. "But it's too late now. That choice has been made for her, like I suspect she's too used to."

Graham nodded absently, his thoughts swirling. He didn't have the energy to argue over burned clothes. Not now. "Let me know if she wakes up. We need to have a conversation. We'll figure out a way to communicate, somehow."

Clarisse nodded, turning back to her patient.

Graham stepped out of the clinic, the tension that had coiled in his chest still wound tight. The cool morning air, a balm on his overheated skin, but it wasn't enough to chase away the unease prickling at the back of his mind.

He glanced around the camp as it slowly came to life. The smell of something cooking—probably oatmeal—wafted from the direction of the communal kitchen, and he caught sight of Olivia and Bethany setting out plates and cups. Olivia worked in silence, her movements precise and controlled, but he noticed the way her shoulders hunched, the tightness around her mouth.

He made his way over, offering a small nod of acknowledgment. "Morning."

"Morning," Olivia murmured, not looking up from the pot she was stirring. "It's going to be a cold one today."

"Feels like it," he agreed. An awkward silence stretched between them, filled only by the crackling of the fire. "How are you holding up?"

Olivia's hand paused mid-stir, and for a second, he thought she was going to brush him off. Then she sighed, setting the ladle down and finally meeting his gaze. "I'm okay. You?"

He just tipped his head.

Her gaze softened, and she offered a small, knowing smile.

"Olivia, just… don't forget to take care of yourself too, okay? Rick would hate to see you like this."

She looked down right away, stirring faster. The mention of Rick sent a fresh wave of grief crashing over her, and Graham swallowed.

Olivia wiped at her eye but didn't look up. "I won't."

He lingered a moment longer, knowing he'd made it worse but also not knowing how to make it better. So he turned and made his way to the radio room, instead.

Macy looked up as he stepped inside, her expression tight with frustration. "They're still not giving us anything useful," she said without preamble. "It's like talking to a brick wall. Or worse—a wall that's high as a kite."

"What's the latest?"

"Something about shadows and veils again," Macy muttered, raking a hand through her short blond hair. "*And beware the breath of the island.* I swear, they're all losing it over there."

"Keep trying." Graham knew it was a hollow command, but it was all he had to offer.

"I am!" Macy snapped, turning to face him fully. "But you know what? It's not like I can pull answers out of thin air! I'm not Rick, okay?"

Graham flinched, the accusation stinging more than he'd expected. "I know you're not," he murmured. "I'm sorry I'm putting so much pressure on you, Macy."

Her shoulders slumped, and she let out a long, shaky breath. "I'm trying, Graham. I really am."

"I know." He took a step closer, his voice softer. "Just… keep me updated. And take a break if you need to. You've got all the connections."

Macy nodded slowly, a shadow of some unreadable emotion flickering across her face. "Yeah. Okay."

Graham turned away, a glare hanging between them. He left the radio room, feeling more drained than before. If the rest of the day proceeded like this, it was going to be a total loss.

CHAPTER 2- SHADOWS ON THE HORIZON

Sam entered the clinic quietly, his gaze sweeping over the unconscious girl on the bed. The bandages on her face and arms starkly contrasted with her olive skin, making the scene almost surreal. She looked fragile, like a broken doll—helpless and lost.

His jaw clenched as he leaned to the side, arms crossed tightly over his chest.

"What is it, Sam? I can't believe you burned her clothes," Clarisse said, not looking up from her notes.

"I know. You can be mad, and I don't care. We need to tie her wrists, too," he said flatly, cutting straight to the point.

Clarisse looked up, a flash of surprise crossing her face before it settled into a frown. "Tie her wrists? Sam, she's just a girl. She has a broken arm, and she can barely move."

"Do I really have to remind you. It was just a girl who nearly ended you and Kade just over a week ago. *This* girl has been through God knows what and might not see us as friends," he replied, his tone steady but firm. "You remember Meg? We let our guard down, and it nearly cost us everything. We're not having that same debate again."

Clarisse's gaze dropped to her own shoulder, the pain of Meg's bullet wound flaring there and her side. And then she looked to the cot on the far wall, where the light didn't reach. Kade still recovering from the awful concussion that nearly took his life. "Meg… right," she whispered, voice tight.

"We gave Meg everything," Sam continued, voice harsh, tinged with bitterness. "We fed her, protected her, and treated her like one of our own. And she repaid us with blood." His gaze shifted to the unconscious girl. "What if this girl tries something? What if we're caught off guard again? We can't let that happen. I won't allow it."

Clarisse sighed, the tension in her shoulders evident. She glanced at the girl's face—so young, so broken. The thought of binding her like a prisoner felt wrong, but Sam's words… he wasn't wrong. Meg's betrayal was a reminder of the lesson they'd learned the hard way.

"She's unconscious, Sam. She can't hurt anyone right now."

"Exactly. Now's the time to do it. What happens if she wakes up and decides we're the enemy with our backs turned? We have to be ready, Clarisse. It's for her safety and ours."

Clarisse shook her head slowly. "I won't tie her up like some animal when she can't even move. We can keep watch for now, but we won't take her dignity away. Not unless we have to. Or we're no better than them."

Sam exhaled sharply, clearly torn. "This isn't about dignity. It's about survival."

"I know we have to treat every new person like a potential threat, but what does that say about us?" Clarisse countered gently. "If we tie up every injured stranger because we're afraid, what makes us different from the people we're fighting against?"

Sam looked away, jaw tight, the lines on his face deepening. "That we're not foolish, for one. That we learned the lesson and we don't need to learn it again. That's what it means."

"We've got to be better than that, Sam."

For a moment, they stood in silence. Finally, Sam nodded reluctantly. "I'm not taking any chances with her. When she's capable of moving, she's a threat. And I want her secured."

"Then we'll handle it," Clarisse said softly, turning back to the girl.

Without another word, Sam turned and walked out of the clinic, leaving Clarisse alone with her thoughts and the fragile figure on the bed.

Sam made his way through the camp, his shoulders tense, thoughts still lingering on the girl in the clinic. The early morning sun cast a pale glow over the cluster of makeshift tents that made up their small community that sprung up around the quarantine units in the first days after the chemical threat was over. Everything was quiet, the camp still stirring to life, but Sam's mind was a storm of worry and frustration.

He found himself outside the small cabin that Bang and Addy now called home. Steeling himself, he pushed the door open gently and stepped inside

Addy was sitting up in a cot, the soft glow of a lantern casting warm light over her long brown hair and the baby cradled in her arms. Bang looked up from where he was crouched beside them, his eyes shadowed with fatigue but brightening at the sight of Sam.

"Hey," Bang greeted quietly, careful not to wake the sleeping infant.

"Hey," Sam replied, his gaze softening as he looked at the baby. Tiny, delicate, and so very fragile. "How's Grae doing this morning?"

Addy smiled, glancing down at her son. "He's perfect. Slept through the night again."

"That's a good boy," Sam murmured, stepping closer and looking down at his grandson. He could still remember the first time he'd heard the name—a week ago. It had taken him by surprise, and the rush of emotions that had overwhelmed him back then still caught him off guard now.

Grae-Samuel-Ho.

Bang and Addy had chosen the name thoughtfully, each part a testament to the people who had shaped their lives. "Grae" for Graham, the man who had been Bang's father and mentor; "Samuel" for himself, Addy's steadfast protector;

and "Ho," the family name Bang had inherited from his Korean birth parents.

"You've got a big name to live up to, little man," Sam whispered, his voice soft and full of affection. He reached out, brushing a finger gently over the baby's tiny hand. Grae's fingers twitched, curling around Sam's finger for a moment before relaxing again. "But I know you're up for it."

Bang shifted slightly, watching Sam closely. "He's lucky to have you as a grandfather, Sam."

Sam shook his head, a small, self-deprecating smile playing at his lips. "I think it's the other way around. I'm the lucky one." He glanced at Bang, then at Addy. "You two are doing a great job."

Addy looked down at Grae, her expression softening even further. "We just want him to be safe, dad."

Sam nodded, understanding the unspoken fear behind her words. "I'm working on it. I promise you that."

Sam stayed for a while longer, just watching the peaceful rise and fall of Grae's tiny chest. There was so much darkness in the world now, so much pain and suffering. But in this moment, in this tent, there was light, too. There was hope.

Finally, Sam straightened, brushing a gentle kiss on the top of Grae's head. "I should go check on the others. Keep me posted if you need anything."

Addy nodded, her gaze following him as he turned to leave. "Dad?"

He paused, glancing back.

"Thank you," she said quietly, her eyes shining. "For everything."

Sam's chest tightened, but he managed a small smile. "Always."

As he stepped out of the cabin, the morning sun began to rise fully over the camp, casting warm light across everything. Despite their looming enemies, despite losing Rick and all the other before him, Sam felt like there was hope. True, real hope. He swore to himself, right then and there, that he would do whatever it took to make sure this family—his family—would not only survive but thrive in this brutal world. They had to. Because there was a future worth fighting for.

CHAPTER 3- A RECKONING OF FATE

Clarisse shifted on the stool beside Kade's cot, leaning forward with her head propped on one hand the other arm in a sling, watching the slow rise and fall of his chest. The soft light from a lantern cast a warm, flickering glow over his face, highlighting the dark smudges beneath his eyes and the slight furrow in his brow. He hadn't had a seizure in two days. That was progress, but his condition was still precarious.

The camp outside was stirring to life, the muted sounds of a morning routine filtering in through the canvas walls of the clinic. Clarisse should have felt relief, but a tension still knotted deep in her chest. Maybe because the stillness meant time to think, and thinking meant confronting all the things she'd been avoiding.

Things like the fact that her injuries were going to take time to heal, and she hated not being physically capable if danger were to arise at a moment's notice. Or that Corey, sensing her vulnerability, had practically moved in with her and the kids without so much as a word of discussion. It wasn't like her to let someone else make decisions about her life, yet here she was, trying to convince herself that it was just temporary. It was better this way—better to have someone close, someone she could lean on. At least, that's what she told herself.

Beside her, Kade shifted restlessly in his sleep, a faint whimper escaping his lips. Clarisse leaned forward, placing a cool hand on his forehead. "It's okay, Kade," she murmured softly. "You're safe. You're okay."

He quieted under her touch, his breathing evening out again. She sat back, letting out a breath she hadn't realized she was holding. This constant state of alertness, of waiting for the other shoe to drop, was exhausting. But it was all she knew how to do. After Dalton's death and Meg's betrayal, after Rick… She shook her head, forcing herself to stay in the present.

The flap of the tent shifted, and Clarisse looked up as Elara entered, carrying a small clay bowl of herbs and roots. "I made more tea," Elara said quietly, setting the bowl on the table beside the cot. "It should help with his seizures."

Clarisse nodded, glancing at the concoction. "Thank you. He's been better the past couple of days."

Elara gave a small, tentative smile. "That's good. I thought… well, I'd stay here today, if that's okay with you. To help. I think Bethany likes working alone."

It wasn't a question, but there was a hint of uncertainty in

Elara's tone that made Clarisse soften. "I'd appreciate that," she said gently. "It'll give me a chance to check on the patients."

"You mean our other patient," Elara corrected, her gaze shifting to the still figure on the cot a few feet away. The swelling in the girl's face had gone down a little, revealing more of her delicate features than the day before. She looked so young, and for the first time since they'd brought her here, Clarisse wondered what kind of life she'd had before they found her. Had they tried to marry her off to some old guy? Is that why she was beaten? It was a common problem in their society. A woman was still treated as a commodity to be traded. How had the world allowed this to continue to the point where one society, with distorted ideas of humanity, be allowed to conquer the globe?

"Any change?" Elara asked softly.

Clarisse shook her head. "No. She hasn't woken up yet. But I think she's close. Her breaths are more frequent."

Elara nodded, moving to the girl's bedside and checking the bandages. "You know, I could make a salve for these wounds. It might ease her pain a bit when she does wake up."

"Do it." Clarisse hesitated, then added, "I was thinking… Sam's right. We don't know if she'll see us as friendly. And after what happened with Meg, I can't take any more risks."

Elara's hands stilled for a moment, then she nodded slowly. "I understand. She's been through so much already. Maybe if she sees we're not like them—"

"Maybe." Clarisse sighed, rubbing a hand over her eyes.

"But we can't assume. Not anymore. I've made that mistake before and it cost us dearly, as you know."

Elara turned back to the girl, gently adjusting the blanket around her shoulders. "I'll keep an eye on her," she murmured, almost to herself. "I won't let anything happen."

Clarisse's chest tightened. "You can't be here all the time, Elara. You need rest too. We all do."

Elara's gaze flickered up to hers, a shadow of something dark and haunted passing through her eyes. "Rest doesn't come easy anymore. Not after Boise. Not after losing all of them." She turned away, fiddling with the edge of the blanket. "This place… It's different. But the grief is the same. I just… I need to be useful. That's all."

Clarisse wanted to reach out, to say something comforting, but the words stuck in her throat. What comfort could she offer when she didn't even have it for herself? Instead, she simply nodded and turned her attention back to Kade.

The tent flap shifted again, and Clarisse looked up to see Paige standing in the entrance, her expression as closed off and wary as ever. But there was a new vulnerability in her eyes, something that hadn't been there before the pregnancy. It made Clarisse's heart ache.

"Checking on the girl?" Clarisse asked, keeping her tone light.

Paige nodded slowly, her gaze drifting over to their new visitor's battered form. "Yeah. Just… wanted to see if I recognized her."

Clarisse studied her for a moment, then stood. "Why don't you come sit? I could use the company."

Paige hesitated, then moved slowly to the cot beside the girl's, sitting down stiffly. She stared at the girl for a long moment, her hands clasped tightly in her lap. "Still a lot of swelling. She looks like... she's been through a lot," Paige murmured finally.

"She has." Clarisse's gaze softened. "Like you were. I was thinking... maybe you could help me talk to her. When she wakes up. If she wakes up. I know you don't know much Arabic, but you might understand more than I would."

Paige's hands tightened around each other, the knuckles turning white. "I don't know. I haven't... I haven't been around them since... since then."

Clarisse reached out, laying a hand gently over Paige's. "You don't have to decide now. But if you're willing, I think it could help. Maybe for both of you."

Paige didn't respond, but the way her shoulders tightened told Clarisse maybe not.

But then Paige stood and reached for a nearby sheet. "Do you need this?"

Knowing what Paige was about to do and also knowing it didn't matter whether she needed the sheet or not, she simply shook her head.

Paige nodded, nicked one edge of the hem with her pocketknife and ripped a long thin strip of fabric.

Elara glanced up and Clarisse just smiled.

But then Kade suddenly pushed up and said, "What is that noise?"

Clarisse hurried to his side, "Kade, don't get up."

"Oh, sorry, Kade," Paige said before ripping another thin strip.

Clarisse tried pushing Kade's shoulders back to the bed.

Kade brushed at his eyes, trying to focus. "What is she doing over there?"

"Lay down. It's fine. We just needed some fabric strips."

"Who is that in the bed. Is that Meg?"

Fabric ripping again.

Clarisse stilled suddenly realizing then, he didn't know. They had the discussion the day before, the one where she told him again the Meg had died. That Rueben was dead too and that Rick had also passed away. And here he was asking for Meg again. What did it mean? Was the concussion worse than she realized?

Kade stopped and looked her in the eyes. "Don't look at me like that. I just…I just had a dream. I know what happened. I remember."

Another rip of fabric.

She nodded quickly. Did he really? "Okay."

"Do you think I could get up and go to the bathroom by myself? I'm sick of lying in this damn bed. And I know you guys are slipping some kind of sedative in that tea. I don't want it."

"Hey," Clarisse said. "You don't need to get upset. I'll get Sam or someone to help you."

Kade pushed his legs over the side of the bed. "I don't need a babysitter to the can."

Clarisse moved her arms out. "Kade, wait."

"What?" he stopped.

Maybe she was overreacting, being overly cautious with his care. "Take it slow, please."

Kade rolled his eyes but slowed when walking past the girl in the bed. "Paige, why are you tying her up? You know, never mind. I don't want to know."

That's when Corey suddenly appeared in the doorway and Clarisse motioned to him to follow Kade.

To her relief, Corey caught on instantly and gave her a thumbs up discreetly as Kade walked past him and struck up a conversation.

"Well, that went well," Elara said.

"We can't blame him. We kept him down as long as we could. It's a good sign really."

Paige came over after finishing her job. "Sorry about the noise, but I really needed to know she wasn't a threat to anyone."

Clarisse chuckled. "We were going to do it, but Sam will be happy to know it's done."

"Good. Now you'll have to make room in your tent for Kade, I suppose. We have Tehya and Cheryl in one tent beside ours. Worries me to have them separate at night though."

Clarisse shifted her stance, not sure what Paige was getting at. "I think Tehya could probably handle any problems, given her recent history."

Paige smirked. "Even the best of us can't keep watch in our sleep. No, what I mean is, would you oppose Kade bunking with the girls? There's room for one more."

"I um, hadn't thought of that. I'm not sure he would go for that either," Clarisse scratched her head.

"Well, he's like their brother. And let's face it, there's not a lot of young men his age for him to bunk with. I mean, Mark and McCann are married and living in their own tents. I just thought it was a practical solution."

"Let me think about that. I'll talk to him. You're right, we don't have a lot of options and the kids, and I and Corey, are crammed in our tent. And well, I'm not sure Kade will be all that thrilled with the situation. But let me see where he stands before I spring that on him."

Elara laughed. "Yeah, he's not exactly in a good mood now. Let's maybe wait on that one."

CHAPTER 4- BENEATH AN INK SKY

Graham watched from afar, chewing on a toothpick that Macy had found—God knows where—as Kade, in a crumpled T-shirt and pajama pants that made him look as if he'd just woken from a mental ward, slipped his feet into boots outside the med tent and stomped off to the latrine that Sam had set up down the hill. All the while, Corey was talking as he followed the boy. It was obvious why Corey was following him, and equally obvious that Kade wanted none of it. He appeared to be moving down the hill as fast as gravity would allow, without actually running. Either he really had to go, or, Graham suspected, he was simply tired of the nursing. Corey made a poor nurse.

The latrine door slammed shut with Kade inside, and Corey stopped about ten feet away. Graham couldn't help but shake his head and laugh a little. "Ri..." Then he remembered. What was once so easily said, now brought the sharp edge of grief. He wanted to give Rick a play-by-play, as if he were sitting in the radio room while Graham peeked around the corner. He wanted to tell him how much he missed him. The thought wiped away Graham's momentary smile. He pulled the toothpick away, broke it in half, and tossed it to the ground and rubbed it into the mud with the toe of his worn leather boot.

"I got something!" Macy yelled through the door flap.

Graham entered the comms tent. "Something good, I hope?"

Macy slid the earphones down to hang around her neck. "I'll let you decide." She picked up the notepad and used her pen to point at something on the page. "So, your contact—the one Tehya has the hots for—"

Graham shook his head. "Don't say it like that."

"You know what I mean. He went over to Bellingham to hang out with the stoners, to decipher what they were trying to say, and got back to me."

"Did he see something from Deception Pass?" Graham, suddenly on edge, felt his heart rate pick up. Had they been spotted leaving the island? Were they on their way to annihilate them now?

"Arlen mentioned the resupply route to Orcas. I mean, they don't often leave the island, but they do receive supplies. And, well, new prisoners."

"And?" Graham found himself impatient, waving his hand to urge Macy to continue."

"And don't rush me—it's a lot," she said, glaring. "One boat arrives every few weeks. But here—Arlen is standing by and wants to tell you." She stood, pulling the earphones from her neck and holding them out to Graham with a roll of her eyes.

"Well, why didn't you say so in the first place? I didn't know he was there." Graham took her place behind the desk and slipped on the warmed earphones. He was never the one to man the radio desk and felt out of place in Macy's seat. "You there? Arlen. Over."

Macy tsked.

"Hey, Graham. Yes, I'm here," a deep voice replied—a voice that sounded like it should belong to an older, wiser man, but instead came from the skinny kid Graham had only recently met and too recently trusted with his rebellious daughter.

Graham nodded. It was nice to hear him, though his voice always came across as calming and poetic. "Macy tells me you've spotted movement near Orcas Island."

"Yes. I've seen this same sailboat before, but not in a long while. It moves like a shadow on the water—silent, deliberate, and patient. The hull is dark, weathered by time and tide, streaked with the scars of a hundred storms. Its sails are as black as raven feathers, catching the faintest whisper of wind, carrying it forward with purpose. Rough markings on its side make it seem like a ghost adrift in the currents—like it doesn't belong to this world anymore. But you can't mistake it for something lost. The Revenant knows exactly where it's going. Its masts rise like bare tree trunks stripped of life, and there's always a hint of something heavy in its wake, as if it's dragging secrets behind it. It carries more than supplies though—something darker, lives stolen from ports like ours.

"I've seen it too often now, coming and going like a predator stalking its range. It's not just a boat; it's a harbinger. Always coming back. Always taking. Never giving. A vulture of the seas."

Graham raised an eyebrow at Macy, who stood there smiling. He held the mic away and whispered, "Has he been partaking with the locals?"

Macy shrugged.

"So, you're saying this sailboat has black sails and is called the Revenant? And that you've seen it around but not for a while? And sometimes it carries a heavy load. Do I have that right?"

"Yes. And at times it's pulling a small barge. It makes sense. There's plenty of wind in the Sound and not a lot of fuel to go around. It goes from port to port. I've seen it docked in Seattle, Port Townsend—here and there. But it's the only boat I've seen that approaches Orcas Island. They have a few security boats monitoring their shores, but they don't bring supplies."

"It all comes down to fuel."

"Yes, and the Revenant has the wind."

"So it really only needs a little fuel to get around. You think it's their supply ship? And sometimes they have a barge?"

Silence.

"Arlen, you there?"

"I've got to go, my friend. There's something happening

here."

"Trouble? Is anything wrong?"

"No. Someone just brought food. We'll speak again soon."

Graham set the mic down on the desk. "And that's it, I guess."

"Munchies. That's my guess," Macy said.

"Is Arlen a stoner too?"

Macy shrugged again. "When in Rome?"

"Geez, we're in the hands of stoners. That's where we're getting our intel." Graham switched places with Macy behind the desk.

"Yeah. What is the world coming to?"

"What do you mean?"

Both of their heads turned when they heard Tehya in the doorway. "What's going on?"

Graham stared at his daughter for a beat. But it was Macy who said what he was thinking.

"Your dad doesn't want you hanging out with Arlen anymore, is my guess."

Tehya chuckled and crossed her arms over her chest. "Arlen. What, did you talk to him?"

God, Macy's right, my daughter has the hots for a stoner hippie dufus who might just be our only link to ending the final vestiges of this cancer once and for all.

Macy stopped flipping through her notes and gawked at him.

He should say something. But he couldn't tear his eyes from his daughter. She was so grown up. Her expression so looked the same on her mother, years ago, when he knew there was something more between them than friendship in a world gone wrong.

"Dad. You're being weird. What?" Tehya splayed her arms out.

Graham snapped out of it and ran a hand through his hair. "Nothing." He turned to Macy. "Do you have the date he last mentioned seeing the Revenant?"

"That's what I'm looking for. But I'll call him back in an hour or so and ask the question again, directly."

"You mean, Arlen?" Tehya said. "I can ask…"

Graham and Macy both said in unison, "No!"

Graham brushed past his daughter by the doorway. He needed to get his head straight and make a plan. That's what Rick would say. *Now's not the time.* And he would be right. But he couldn't help but mutter on his way to find the others, "God I hope the next one's a boy."

But the moment he walked out the door, he began to run toward the clinic, because Clarisse shouted his name.

"What? What is it?"

Paige met him at the door, her face pale, her eyes, sharp with distain. "The girl. She's awake. It's not what we thought."

Graham glanced passed Paige as others showed up at the door behind him, curious about the commotion. Elara held a cup to the girl's mouth, encouraging her to take a sip. The child's eyes so swollen he couldn't imagine she could see a thing.

Sam on the other side of the girl, undoing the binds that held the girl to the bed. "I was wrong. I'm sorry."

The girl bobbed her head but pulled away from Sam the moment her wrist was free.

Clarisse looked upset as she approached him shaking her head.

"What's happening here?" Graham asked but she looked as if she was about to cry.

Clarisse cleared her throat. Placed her hands on her hips. "She's not Arabic, Graham. She's not one of them. The girl's Hawaiian. She's American."

"Are you saying…."

"They took her." Paige spat out.

Graham pulled in a deep breath. "Same story. How old is she? How long…."

"We don't have all the answers yet." Clarisse said. "She's thinks she's fourteen. She doesn't know for sure or where her parents are. She said it's been years since she was taken from the islands when she was only ten."

"Are we sure?" Graham stared at the girl again who had curled up on her side away from Sam and toward Elara.

"She has the accent," Clarisse said rubbing her arm.

"Still, we have to be careful. Just like Meg, could have been converted," Paige said.

Graham shook his head, his mind flashing on the girl being beaten in the courtyard as he walks by. His throat closed up. He did nothing. Used the beating as a diversion to sneak by. "What are her injuries? Will she recover?"

Clarisse pushed her glasses up the bridge of her nose. "Physically, she'll recover in time. She took a severe beating.

Had you guys not taken her, she might have died there. Mentally…"

Paige interrupted. "She'll get over it. We'll help her." Paige grabbed his shoulder sleeve. "Come on. Let's talk."

Before he followed, he motioned to Clarisse. "Keep me updated."

She nodded, "Of course."

When he turned around, most of the camp stood behind him with silent questions, including his daughter.

"We heard most of it," Teyha said. "Is she the same as Meg?"

"We don't know. Let's give Clarisse time to get her well. Everyone get back to your posts."

Mark said what everyone was thinking. "When are we going back? What about Lawoaka and the others?"

"We're getting to that," Paige said. "Now, let's not make it easy for them. Everyone, get back to where you belong. Aren't you on duty, Cheryl?"

"Yes, but…."

"No buts."

Graham wasn't sure what Paige was going on about but sensed there was something urgent and she needed the privacy to tell him just what that was.

"Is it the girl? What's going on?" he whispered as she urged him back to their tent. He stepped in behind her and she slapped the flap closed behind them. In the darkness he could feel her hard breath.

"Graham."

He pulled her closer. "Are you not feeling well? Is it the baby?"

She leaned her head into his chest, rubbing her forehead back and forth. "It's…no."

"Paige. Tell me what's going on?"

"I can't. What are we doing. That girl. These people. It could have Tehya or Cheryl."

He pulled in a deep breath. Let it out slow. This was worry. That's all it was. This was normal. This he could deal with. He remembered his first wife going through the same thing. Nelly. And their unborn child. That was all he'd allow his mind to bear after all this time.

He wrapped his hand gently around the back of her neck and whispered, "But it wasn't Cheryl or Tehya. And it won't be this child we've made between us, either."

"You can't just say that, Graham. That girl in there. She had parents. She's been violated since she was ten years old and nearly died had you not stumbled by. They would have killed her like they've done so many. I was…."

"Shh." He pulled her closer as he felled her come to tears. She'd never spoken of her captivity with the terrorists. He assumed the worst. She didn't need to relive it. She did what she had to do to keep Cheryl from the same fate.

"I don't know why I'm so upset," Paige sobbed.

"Surprise, you're human," he smiled a little and kissed her on the top of the head. "It's the hormones."

"I don't like it. I don't like feeling vulnerable."

"I know that about you, but understand you made me a

promise. No disappearing. I need to know where you are at all times, Paige."

She nodded against his chest.

He moved his hand along her jaw and lifted her chin until her blurry eyes looked up in the dim light to his. "I love you, Paige. You're not alone anymore. We're a family. I need to protect you."

"I'm trying to get used to that."

"I know. For now, you need to trust me."

"I do, trust you."

He lowered his lips to hers and kissed her then. First slow, because she was scared, and Paige was never scared, and then a little harder because she pulled him deeper, and he wasn't about to resist her. Not after she gave him her trust.

CHAPTER 5- THE SUDDEN SHIFT

The sky at Deception Pass was inky black, the sliver of a moon casting silver streaks across the calm waters. Stars blinked down from the heavens, their faint glow reflected on the rippling waves. It was the kind of night that could swallow secrets, where shadows melted into the trees and whispers carried farther than footsteps.

Tehya sat on a flat rock near the water's edge, her arms wrapped around her knees, gazing at the quiet expanse of the Sound. The salty air mixed with the scent of the evergreens behind her, but no matter how peaceful it seemed, the tension in the air was undeniable. Every rustle of leaves or crack of a branch had her heart racing. Something was wrong, but she couldn't name it.

Marcy sat a few feet away, her posture stiff and unyielding, hands folded neatly in her lap. She hadn't said much since they arrived the day before, her gaze distant. Tehya found herself glancing at her sister, trying to piece together the change in her. Marcy was usually steady, reliable. She seemed distracted—no, preoccupied.

Behind them, Mark and McCann were near the truck, checking their weapons again. The quiet metallic clicks of magazines being loaded and chamber checks being made carried through the still air. Graham stood with them, murmuring in low tones, his silhouette etched against the dim glow of their lantern.

Corey paced along the shore, his eyes fixed on the horizon, scanning for any sign of Arlen and the boat they were counting on. The plan was straightforward- sail across the Sound under the cover of night and reach the Seattle port before dawn. But Tehya knew better than to trust that things would go as planned.

A flicker of movement on the water caught her attention. Tehya stood, squinting into the dark. The small boat appeared almost ghostly, its hull blending into the black waves, the only giveaway the glint of moonlight off the prow. Arlen's familiar figure stood at the helm, guiding the craft steadily toward them.

"Arlen's here!" Corey called softly, waving to the others.

The group gathered near the shoreline, their movements quiet and deliberate. The hum of the boat's engine grew louder as Arlen brought it closer, cutting through the water with practiced ease.

Tehya stole another glance at Marcy, expecting her to remain composed and distant. But to her surprise, Marcy suddenly straightened, her gaze locking onto Arlen with a newfound intensity. Her lips parted slightly, and for the first time since they left camp, her expression softened.

"Marcy?" Tehya whispered, confusion creeping into her voice.

Marcy didn't respond. Her eyes remained glued to Arlen as he secured the boat to the dock and stepped off. There was a confidence to his movements, a quiet authority that made Tehya uneasy. But it wasn't Arlen's presence that unsettled her. It was the way Marcy was looking at him—like he was more than just a passing ally.

"Good to see you," Graham greeted Arlen, stepping forward to shake his hand.

"You too," Arlen replied, his gaze sweeping over the group before landing on Tehya and then on Marcy. He lingered there, something unspoken passing between them. His lips quirked into a small smile, and Marcy returned it—a brief, almost shy expression that Tehya had never seen from her before.

What the hell is going on? Tehya wondered, her brow furrowing.

"We should move quickly," Arlen said, tearing his gaze away from Marcy. "The moon's bright tonight, but we need to be across the Sound before first light."

Corey nodded. "Let's load up."

As the group moved to gather supplies, Tehya found herself watching Marcy and Arlen again. They stood close but didn't speak. Arlen's gaze softened as he looked at her, and Marcy's usual guarded demeanor seemed to melt away.

Tehya clenched her jaw, feeling a knot tighten in her chest.

It wasn't jealousy. It was confusion—and a creeping sense of unease. What was happening between them? And why hadn't she noticed it before?

Before she could dwell on it, a sudden crack of gunfire shattered the quiet night.

"Get down!" Graham barked, pulling his rifle from his shoulder.

Tehya dropped to the ground, her heart pounding in her chest. The gunfire echoed through the pass, coming from the direction of the tree line. Shadows moved between the trees, figures darting in and out of sight.

"Who the hell is that?" McCann growled, his eyes narrowing as he scanned the dark forest.

"I don't know," Graham replied, his voice tense. "But we've got to move. Now."

Mark was already at the boat, helping Corey secure the supplies. "We need to push off!"

Tehya's mind raced. Marcy was still crouched beside her, her eyes wide with fear. Arlen stood protectively in front of her, his hand resting on the hilt of a knife at his belt.

"Tehya!" Graham's voice cut through the chaos, sharp and commanding. "Get to the boat!"

She scrambled to her feet, grabbing Marcy's arm. "Come on! We've got to go!"

Marcy hesitated for a moment, her gaze flickering to Arlen. He gave her a nod, his expression steady. "Go. I'll cover you."

"No," Marcy said firmly. "Not without you."

Arlen's lips pressed into a thin line, but he didn't argue. He grabbed her hand, pulling her toward the boat.

Tehya ran ahead, her heart pounding in her ears. The sound of gunfire grew louder, bullets striking the ground around them. She ducked and weaved, adrenaline surging through her veins.

As she reached the dock, she heard Graham's voice again, yelling her name.

"Tehya! Hurry!"

She turned to see him standing near the tree line, his rifle raised. McCann and Mark were already on the boat, urging the others to move faster.

Tehya glanced back at Marcy and Arlen. They were almost there, but the gunfire was relentless. Shadows moved closer, the figures emerging from the trees with weapons drawn.

"We're not going to make it!" Marcy yelled, panic creeping into her voice.

"Yes, we will," Arlen replied, his voice calm and steady. "Keep moving."

Tehya reached the boat and turned to help them aboard. Corey grabbed her arm, pulling her onto the deck as the boat rocked beneath them.

"Come on!" Corey shouted. "We've got to go!"

Graham fired a few more shots before retreating toward the dock. Arlen and Marcy were right behind him, their footsteps pounding against the rocks.

Just as they reached the boat, a bullet ricocheted off the rock with a spark. Marcy stumbled, but Arlen caught her, pulling her to her feet.

"Get on!" Graham ordered, his voice fierce.

They climbed aboard, and Corey pushed off. The boat drifted into the water, the engine humming to life.

As they moved away from the shore, the gunfire began to fade. The figures in the trees didn't pursue, but their presence lingered like a shadow over the group.

Tehya collapsed onto the deck, her chest heaving as she caught her breath. Marcy sat beside her, her hands trembling.

"What the hell was that?" Tehya asked, her voice shaky.

Graham crouched beside her, his expression grim. "Trouble."

Corey steered the boat into open water, the waves lapping against the hull. The moonlight shimmered on the surface, guiding their way across the Sound.

Tehya looked at her father, her heart still racing. "What now?"

Graham's gaze hardened, his jaw clenched. "I guess we're losing the truck and you two are coming along after all. Now, we finish what we started."

The boat sailed on, leaving the shore behind. But the danger wasn't over. It was just beginning.

CHAPTER 6- ACROSS THE SOUND

The moon hung high in the sky, a thin crescent that painted streaks of silver across the dark water. The boat cut through the waves, each lurch and swell jarring the passengers inside. Graham sat near the stern, his gaze fixed on the horizon, but his mind lingered on what they had just left behind.

The shoreline of Deception Pass was barely a shadow now, lost in the mist and darkness. The gunfire that had chased them to the boat still echoed in his ears, though the night had long since swallowed the sound. His heart hadn't stopped pounding since they pushed off.

He glanced across the deck. Corey manned the helm, his eyes locked on the dark expanse ahead, his hands steady on the wheel despite the choppy water. Mark sat beside him, double-checking their supplies, while McCann leaned against the railing, his rifle slung across his back. Marcy, Tehya, and Arlen sat huddled near the bow, the three extra passengers they hadn't planned on bringing. The boat was overloaded with equipment and now three additional passengers, and every wave seemed to remind them of that fact. The added weight made the ride rougher, and Graham could feel it in every lurch of the vessel.

The wind was biting, cutting through their clothes like icy blades. The men had come prepared for the cold, layered in jackets and scarves, but the girls hadn't. Tehya and Marcy huddled close together, their teeth chattering as they fought to keep warm.

Arlen, standing near the bow, glanced at Marcy. Without a word, he shrugged off his thick jacket and draped it over her shoulders. Marcy looked up, startled, and met his gaze. For a moment, something unspoken passed between them—a lingering glance that made Marcy's cheeks flush, though it was impossible to tell if it was from the cold or something else.

Mark, standing at the helm with Corey, caught the exchange. His jaw clenched, and his hands tightened around the edge of the boat. He said nothing, but Graham noticed the tension in his posture.

Corey adjusted the course, and the boat rocked with the movement. Graham shifted his weight, gripping the edge of the seat to steady himself.

"How's she holding?" he asked Corey.

Corey glanced back, his expression calm but focused. "She's a solid vessel, but she wasn't meant for this much weight. We're sitting lower in the water than I'd like. We'll make it, though."

Graham nodded, trusting Corey's judgment. He had spent years on the water before the world changed, and if anyone could navigate this crossing, it was him.

Mark moved closer, crouching beside Graham. "We've got enough fuel to make it to Port Townsend, but if we hit any trouble, we're cutting it close."

"Let's hope we don't hit trouble," Graham replied, though he knew better than to expect an easy trip.

A sudden swell lifted the boat, and Marcy let out a soft gasp as she gripped the railing. Tehya steadied her, placing a hand on her sister-in-law's arm.

"Are you all right?" Tehya asked quietly.

Marcy nodded, but her gaze remained distant. "I'm fine."

Graham watched the interaction, his brow furrowing. What was going on between them? Marcy hadn't once looked at Mark since they boarded the boat. Instead, her focus seemed to drift to Arlen every time he moved.

He stood and made his way to the bow, sitting beside Tehya. She glanced at him but said nothing.

"You holding up?" he asked.

Tehya shrugged. "I'm here."

"That's not what I asked."

She sighed, resting her chin on her knees. "I'm fine, Dad. Just… tired."

Graham studied her for a moment. He could see the exhaustion in her eyes, but there was something else—something she wasn't saying.

"I didn't want you to come," he said softly.

"I know."

"But you're here now. And I need to know you're ready for this."

Tehya met his gaze, her expression serious. "I'm ready. I know what we're up against if that's what you're asking."

Graham nodded slowly. He wanted to believe her, but the image of her running from gunfire was still fresh in his mind, sitting right next to the image of her slicing through Meg's throat.

A sudden shout from Corey drew their attention. "Lights on the horizon!"

Graham stood, moving to the helm. Corey pointed toward the distance, where a faint glow broke through the darkness.

"Patrol boat?" Graham asked.

"Could be," Corey replied. "It's moving slow, but it's definitely out there."

McCann joined them, his hand resting on his rifle. "We can't risk being seen."

"We'll adjust course," Corey said, turning the wheel slightly. "Take us farther out into the Sound. It'll add time, but it'll keep us out of sight."

Graham nodded in agreement. "Do it."

As the boat shifted direction and the waves grew rougher, Graham glanced back at Tehya and Marcy. They huddled closer to avoid the wind, but he noticed Marcy's eyes flicking toward Arlen again, as if drawn to him by some invisible thread. He shifted uneasily, noting the tension in Mark's posture as he kept his focus ahead. The last thing they needed was tension in the group. The girls were still seated near the bow, their heads close together as they spoke in hushed tones.

He couldn't hear what they were saying, but he could see the concern etched on their faces.

The boat rocked again, the waves growing rougher as they moved farther from shore. The wind picked up, chilling the air even more.

"Keep your eyes peeled," Graham said to McCann. "We don't want any surprises."

McCann nodded, scanning the water with practiced precision.

The night stretched on, each passing hour tightening the tension in the air. The hum of the engine, even muffled, seemed too loud against the crashing waves. Every minute felt stretched and strained, as if the water itself was holding its breath, waiting for the moment they would be spotted. The lights on the horizon faded into the distance, but Graham remained on edge.

Corey glanced at his watch and then out over the water, his expression tense. The boat was heavier than expected with the additional passengers, and it was taking a toll on their speed. "We've been lucky so far, but we can't count on it staying that way. We need to stay in the cover of night. Once the lights ashore go out, we muffle the engine and make the last stretch quietly. If we wait too long, dawn will expose us." The Port Townsend dock loomed in the distance, a ghostly silhouette against the morning light.

"We're getting close," Corey announced, his voice low, his gaze fixed on the horizon. "Another hour at most if we keep our speed and stay out of sight." "Another hour, maybe less."

Graham nodded, but his mind was already on the next

step. They had made it across the Sound, but the real danger was still ahead. The port. The barge. The mission that could change everything.

He glanced back at Tehya one last time. She caught his gaze and offered a small, reassuring smile.

They had made it this far. Now, they had to see it through.

CHAPTER 7- THE BARGE

The water stretched out endlessly, dark and cold, rippling under the faint moonlight. The boat creaked and groaned with each wave, its weight and the tension of its passengers pressing heavily on Graham's mind. He stood near the helm, his eyes scanning the horizon, searching for a sign—any sign—that this journey wouldn't be in vain.

Corey steered with a steady hand, his focus unwavering despite the rough waters. Graham trusted Corey's instincts on the sea, but tonight, everything felt precarious. The stakes were higher. The people with him weren't seasoned warriors—they were family. His family. His daughter.

Graham's gaze drifted toward Tehya, who sat near the bow with Marcy and Arlen. They huddled together against the cold, their faces drawn and weary. Tehya hadn't spoken much since they boarded the boat, her expression a mix of determination and unease. She had grown so much in the past few years, hardened by the world they lived in. But she was still his little girl, and the thought of her being in harm's way twisted his gut.

Arlen stood at the bow, his sharp eyes scanning the water. Suddenly, he stiffened, raising a hand to signal Corey. "There," he said, pointing toward the distant shore. "I see it. The barge."

Graham followed Arlen's gaze and saw the silhouette of the barge against the faint glow of the coastline. It moved slowly, its bulk cutting through the water with a quiet menace. A chill ran down his spine.

"That's it?" McCann asked, moving to stand beside Graham. His voice was low, but there was a hint of excitement in it.

"That's it," Arlen confirmed. "They make regular stops at Port Townsend. Supplies, mostly. Sometimes... other things."

Graham frowned. "Other things?"

Arlen glanced back at him, his expression grim. "People."

Silence fell over the boat, the weight of that word settling heavily on everyone. Graham's jaw tightened as he processed the information.

"How do the people of Port Townsend stomach it?" Graham asked, his voice laced with disgust. "Trading with them? Letting them dock and take whatever they want?"

Arlen's eyes darkened. "They don't have a choice. If they refuse, they'll take their daughters. Hell, they've already taken some."

Graham felt a knot form in his stomach. He had always suspected there was more to Port Townsend's reluctance to communicate regularly. Now he knew why. The town wasn't just surviving—it was under siege, quietly held hostage by the very people they were about to face.

"How many?" Graham asked quietly.

Arlen shook his head. "Too many. And those they don't take, they keep in fear. That's why the barge comes at night. They don't want anyone thinking they can resist."

Graham glanced at Marcy and Tehya. The girls had been silent, but their eyes reflected the same horror he felt. Marcy pulled Arlen's jacket tighter around her shoulders, her gaze fixed on the distant barge.

"We can't leave them here," Graham said, his voice firm. "Not in Port Townsend."

Tehya's head snapped up. "What do you mean?"

Graham met her gaze. "We don't know what the situation is in Port Townsend. If they're already compromised, I'm not risking leaving you two behind. It's too dangerous."

Marcy frowned. "But we were supposed to wait with Arlen—"

"Plans change," Graham interrupted. "I won't take the chance."

Tehya crossed her arms over her chest. "So what? You're bringing us on the barge?"

Graham sighed, rubbing a hand over his face. "I don't know yet. But we'll figure it out."

Corey cut the engine, letting the boat drift silently toward the shoreline. The distant lights of Port Townsend blinked out one by one as the town settled into sleep. The barge loomed closer, a hulking shadow against the night sky.

"We're running out of time," Corey said quietly. "If we're going to do this, we need to move soon. Dawn's not far off."

Graham nodded, his mind racing. Every plan he had made felt fragile now, the weight of reality pressing in on all sides. He glanced back at Tehya and Marcy again, his heart aching with the knowledge that he couldn't protect them from everything.

A memory surfaced—one of the early missions, back when it was him, Clarisse, Rick, and Dalton. Back when the world still had some semblance of order. They had been younger then, more reckless. But they had each other's backs. Now, it was different. Now, it was the kids stepping up, carrying the weight of survival on their shoulders.

"What would Tala think of me now?" he muttered under his breath.

McCann heard him and gave a small, understanding nod. "She'd think you're doing what you have to do. Just like always."

Graham grunted, unsure if that was true. He couldn't shake the image of Tala's disapproving glare, her fierce love for Tehya shining through even in their worst moments. He could almost hear her voice, scolding him for taking risks with their daughter's life.

"We'll board the barge when they dock," Graham said, his voice steady despite the turmoil inside him. "Corey, you stay with the boat. Keep it ready. If things go south, we'll need a quick escape."

Corey nodded. "Got it."

Graham turned to Arlen. "You've been on the barge before?"

Arlen shook his head. "No, I've never been on the barge. They don't let outsiders anywhere near it. But I've watched it dock enough times to know their routines."

"Good. Then you'll guide us as far as you can. Once we're aboard, we'll have to figure things out as we go."

Tehya stepped forward, her brow furrowed. "And us? We stay with Corey, right?"

Graham's jaw tightened. "Yes, you stay on the boat with Corey. We can't afford to split too far, but I'm not risking you two on that barge." He didn't want them anywhere near the danger. But he couldn't see a way around it.

"Stay alert and keep the boat ready for a fast getaway," he said. "If things go south, we'll need to move quickly. Corey, that's on you."

Tehya nodded, her expression fierce. Marcy looked less certain, but she squared her shoulders and nodded as well.

Graham glanced at Mark. "You ready?"

Mark grinned, his hand resting on his rifle. "Always."

As the boat bobbed gently, Graham took a deep breath, steeling himself for what was to come. The mission was underway. There was no turning back now.

CHAPTER 8- SILENT CONQUEST

The barge loomed, a dark shadow gliding silently across the moonlit water. Graham squinted, his eyes trained on the silhouette ahead, barely distinguishable from the night sky. Arlen, perched at the front of the small boat, lifted a hand and pointed toward it, his movements deliberate and precise.

"There," Arlen murmured, his voice barely audible over the gentle lapping of the waves. "That's the one."

Graham nodded, his expression set in a grim line. "Corey, slow us down. Let's drift in quietly."

Corey eased back on the throttle, the boat's engine fading to a low hum before cutting out completely. They were gliding now, propelled by momentum and the soft current of the Sound. The quiet was unnerving, every creak of the boat seeming far too loud.

In the silence, McCann shifted beside him, his rifle held loosely but ready. "What's the plan, Graham?"

"We take it quietly. No noise, no mistakes," Graham replied. His gaze flicked to the others. "We can't risk blowing our cover. One shot was already too much."

Mark, seated near the stern, nodded in agreement. "We go in fast, take out anyone on board, and keep the barge on its usual route. No detours."

Graham glanced at Arlen. "You've seen this route before?"

Arlen's jaw tightened, his usual easygoing demeanor replaced by something colder. "Many times. They take this route to Port Townsend for supplies. The locals there have no choice but to trade with them."

"Why?" Tehya asked from the back of the boat, her voice cutting through the tension. Her tone carried more than just curiosity—it carried suspicion.

Arlen's gaze shifted to her, and for a moment, there was something unreadable in his eyes. "Because if they don't, their daughters go missing."

The boat fell into a tense silence. Graham clenched his fists, his mind racing. He had suspected something darker about the supply routes, but hearing it confirmed left a bitter taste in his mouth.

"So they already have them," McCann said grimly, his voice low. "The daughters."

Arlen nodded. "Some, yes. Others… they trade their silence for safety."

Graham took a deep breath, his gaze locked on the barge. The mission felt heavier now, more personal. They weren't just stealing a barge—they were dismantling a system of fear.

"We do this right," Graham said, his voice firm. "No mistakes."

The boat bumped gently against the side of the barge, the impact barely registering. Graham reached up, grabbing hold of the rail and hauling himself over the side. McCann followed closely, his movements swift and practiced. Mark brought up the rear, his footsteps muffled by the damp deck.

The air smelled of salt and oil, a harsh tang that clung to their clothes. The deck was empty, but Graham knew better than to trust appearances.

"McCann, take the bow," Graham whispered. "Mark, cover the stern. Arlen, stay close."

They moved as one, their footsteps ghosting across the deck. Graham's heart pounded in his chest, each beat a reminder of what was at stake. He glanced toward the cabin, its windows dark. There had to be someone inside.

McCann signaled from the bow, indicating two figures. They were seated, their postures relaxed—guarded, but not alert.

Graham crept forward, his pistol drawn. The guards hadn't noticed him yet, their conversation carried out in low, murmuring voices. He moved closer, his steps measured and deliberate.

Then, without warning, one of the guards stood, turning toward him. Their eyes met for a brief second, and Graham saw the flicker of realization.

The guard opened his mouth to yell, but Graham was faster. He lunged forward, clamping a hand over the man's mouth and driving his pistol butt into the side of his head. The guard crumpled to the deck silently.

The second guard barely had time to react before McCann was on him, a swift strike rendering him unconscious.

"Clear," McCann murmured.

Graham nodded, his gaze sweeping the deck. "Mark, check the cabin."

Mark moved quickly, disappearing inside. Moments later, he returned with a grim expression. "Three more inside. All asleep."

Graham considered their options. They couldn't risk these men waking up later. He made a decision.

"Take them out," he said, his voice low but firm.

Mark and McCann nodded, slipping inside with knives drawn. Silence followed, broken only by the barely audible sounds of fabric shifting, a quiet exhale, the final moments of three men who never saw their deaths coming.

Minutes later, Mark emerged, wiping his blade on a cloth. McCann followed, his expression unreadable. "It's done," he said simply.

Graham gave a curt nod, pushing away any lingering thoughts. This was war. There was no room for hesitation.

"Corey, status?" Graham whispered into his radio.

Corey's voice crackled through. "No movement from shore. We're clear."

Relief flooded through Graham. "Good. Keep the engine hot. We'll need to move soon."

Arlen stepped forward, his expression tense. "I know the route. We keep the lights low and stick to the shoreline. They won't notice anything unusual."

Graham glanced toward the dark horizon. The sky was beginning to lighten, dawn creeping closer. They didn't have much time.

"Let's go," he said, moving toward the controls.

The barge moved slowly through the water, its engine a low hum that blended with the gentle lapping of the waves. Graham stood at the helm, his eyes scanning the horizon.

Arlen stood beside him, his gaze locked on the shoreline. "We keep to the right, follow the curve of the land."

Graham nodded. "You've done this before?"

Arlen hesitated, then shook his head with a hint of annoyance. "No. I've seen it done. But like I've said before, I've never been on the barge."

Graham's grip on the wheel tightened. "Then let's hope your observations were accurate."

Behind them, McCann and Mark stood watch, their eyes never leaving the water. The tension was palpable, each man aware of how fragile their cover was.

"Corey," Graham said into the radio. "Any signs of movement?"

"Nothing yet," Corey replied. "Tehya's keeping watch. We're clear."

Graham allowed himself a brief moment of relief. They were on their way, but the hardest part was still ahead.

"Keep your eyes open," he said to Arlen. "We can't afford any surprises."

Arlen nodded, his gaze steady. "I know."

The barge glided through the water, a ghost in the night. They were on borrowed time, each passing second bringing them closer to discovery.

Graham glanced toward the horizon, where the first hints of dawn were beginning to show.

"Let's hope we make it before sunrise," he murmured.

Behind him, Mark chuckled softly.

CHAPTER 9- ACROSS THE WATER

The night stretched out over the water like a thick, silent curtain, the only sounds the rhythmic lapping of waves against the hull of the boat Corey piloted. Tehya sat in the stern, her knees drawn up against her chest, arms wrapped around them as she watched the silhouette of the stolen barge ahead. Graham and the others had taken it without a hitch, slipping through the darkness like ghosts. Now, they were on their way to Port Townsend, moving slowly, following the same route the barge always took to avoid raising suspicion.

Tehya exhaled, her breath visible in the frigid air. The temperature had dropped sharply the moment they left Deception Pass. She hadn't been prepared for it, not like the men were. Graham, McCann, and Mark had anticipated the cold, layering up with waterproof gear. Even Corey had been smart enough to wear something warm. But Tehya and

Marcy had not, and now the cold was beginning to seep into her bones.

Marcy shivered beside her, hugging her arms. Corey, sitting at the helm, noticed. Without hesitation, he shrugged off his heavy jacket and handed it to her. "Here. Take it."

Marcy hesitated but took the jacket and slipped it on.

The boat bobbed with the waves, its small size making every shift of the water feel exaggerated. Tehya tried to steady herself, but the relentless, rolling motion made her stomach twist. She clenched her jaw and swallowed hard, willing herself not to be sick. She wasn't used to boats. She wasn't used to any of this. Everything about this mission felt foreign to her—dangerous in a way she wasn't prepared for.

She turned to Corey, who sat at the helm, his hands steady on the wheel. "What's really going on?" she asked. "Why does my dad think saving this girl is so important?"

Corey sighed, his eyes scanning the darkened shoreline as they trailed behind the barge. "It's more than just saving her. It's about making things right."

"Right?" Tehya shook her head. "This whole world is broken. Nothing is right anymore."

Marcy, still wrapped in Corey's jacket, spoke quietly. "I knew Lawoaka's family. Back in Hope, Canada. Before everything."

Tehya turned to her, curious. "You did?"

Marcy nodded. "I was a teenager when I last saw her. She was just a little kid back then. Her sister, Lavinda, was older than her but still younger than me. Their mom…" Marcy trailed off, shaking her head. "She was kind. Strong, like my mom. I remember thinking Lawoaka was lucky to have a mother like that."

"What happened to them?"

Marcy swallowed. "Reuben said, the virus took them. Lavinda and her mom both died."

Tehya's stomach turned. The virus had taken so many, but hearing it put so plainly, so personally, made it hit differently.

"He said he did everything he could to keep Lawoaka safe," Marcy continued. "But he couldn't stop what happened next. They were captured."

"By the terrorists." Tehya finished the thought for her, her voice barely above a whisper.

Marcy nodded. "And you can imagine what that meant for her. A girl. Alone. In their hands."

A chill ran down Tehya's spine that had nothing to do with the cold. She didn't need to ask for details. She could picture them well enough.

"She doesn't even know her father died recently," Marcy said, her voice thick with sorrow. "When we find her… that's going to break her."

Tehya let the words settle, watching the barge up ahead. The men were on board, moving the vessel along its usual course, pretending nothing was out of place. It was a delicate game, one that relied on deception and timing. One mistake, and everything could fall apart.

The silence stretched between them, filled only by the creak of the boat and the low murmur of waves. A sudden gust of wind cut through Tehya's thin jacket, making her shiver. She pulled it tighter around herself, pressing her hands into her arms to generate warmth.

Marcy hesitated before speaking again. "Reuben left the group because he couldn't live with what Clarisse was doing. He didn't agree with her decisions—thought she had become too ruthless, too willing to make sacrifices for the greater good. He wanted something different for his family, a future that didn't mean constant war. So he took his family and left, hoping to outrun the darkness. But it caught up with him anyway."

Tehya let that sink in, feeling a fresh wave of unease settle over her. Everything about this mission, about what they were doing, felt heavier now. She had thought this was just another job, another step in their endless struggle for survival. But it was more than that. It always was.

Corey turned his head slightly, his gaze flickering toward the distant shore. "We're nearly through the channel. The water will open up soon."

Tehya followed his gaze. There were faint torch lights up ahead in the distance, flickering against the dark coastline. The barge was moving at a steady pace, blending in as it should. They were still in the clear. For now.

She shifted uncomfortably, wishing she felt more prepared, more capable. She had spent most of her life in a world dictated by survival, but this—this was something else entirely. A mission with stakes that extended beyond just them.

Tehya pulled her jacket tighter around her. "And after that? What happens next?"

Corey exhaled, his fingers tightening on the wheel. "Then the real work begins."

CHAPTER 10 - THE BARGE DOCKS AT ORCAS

The rhythmic thrum of the barge's engine vibrated beneath Graham's feet as they neared the dock at Orcas Island. The dark water lapped against the hull, the salty sea air mixing with diesel fumes. Everything was on schedule. Too smooth, maybe.

Graham adjusted the strap on his rifle and looked toward Arlen, who had one hand gripping the wheel and the other white-knuckling the radio mic. They had been running dark and silent since Port Townsend, but now, as they approached the dock, the radio suddenly crackled to life.

A garbled voice filled the airwaves, barking something in Arabic.

Arlen's eyes went wide, and for a split second, the entire crew aboard the barge froze.

"Shit," McCann muttered under his breath.

"Answer it," Graham hissed, shoving Arlen toward the mic.

"Answer it?! With what?" Arlen shot back, looking wild-eyed at Graham like he'd just asked him to recite the Quran.

Graham ground his teeth. "You've been listening to their radio chatter this whole time! What do they say when they check in?"

Arlen hesitated, then took a deep breath, pressed the transmit button, and in his best Arabic impression muttered, "Yalla, habibi."

Silence followed.

The radio was still hot. Still open.

Then, laughter crackled back through the speaker.

"Ah-ha-ha! La mushkila!" came the response, followed by more Arabic Graham didn't understand.

Arlen, looking more panicked than ever, choked out another phrase: "Mafi mushkila!"

Another burst of laughter. Then static.

The radio went quiet.

Arlen exhaled loudly, his hands shaking as he put the mic down. "Holy shit."

Graham's head whipped around. "What the hell did you just say?"

Arlen blinked, still pale. "Hell, I don't know. That's just what they say. I think it means 'no problem' or 'all good' or some shit."

McCann let out a dry chuckle. "You just gambled all our lives on 'yalla, habibi'?"

Arlen swallowed, then nodded. "Yeah. Yeah, I did."

Mark grunted. "Damn. That might've been the ballsiest thing I've ever seen."

Arlen gave a weak laugh. "Well, I nearly pissed myself, so there's that."

Graham shook his head and let out a breath. "Okay. We keep moving like nothing happened. Stick to the plan."

The dock was coming up fast now. The steel frame loomed out of the darkness, shadowy figures barely visible moving along the pier. The terrorists weren't expecting trouble. They weren't expecting anything at all.

And that's what made it the perfect moment to strike.

As the barge nudged up against the dock, Graham gave a sharp nod to his team. "We wait. When they board to check the cargo, we take them out quietly. No gunfire unless absolutely necessary."

The first of the terrorists appeared, a single man wearing a mismatched set of fatigues, cradling an AK-47 like it was an afterthought. He stepped onto the ramp, frowning as he scanned the deck.

McCann didn't give him a chance to think twice. He stepped forward from the shadows and buried his knife into the man's throat. A gurgling sound. Then nothing. McCann caught the body before it could slump to the deck and eased it down.

The second terrorist wasn't far behind. He called out something in Arabic, stepping onto the ramp. He stopped when he saw the first man on the ground.

Mark lunged from behind a crate, his own knife flashing

in the dim light. A swift slice across the throat, and the second man crumpled before he could make a sound.

A third terrorist, catching sight of the motion, hesitated at the top of the ramp. Before he could shout an alarm, Graham raised his suppressed pistol and fired a single shot. The man collapsed where he stood.

Three down. No alarm.

They waited, muscles tense, watching for more. Nothing.

The dock remained still.

Graham turned to Arlen. "Stay with the barge. If anything goes south, you take off. No heroics."

Arlen nodded. "You got it."

Graham motioned to McCann and Mark. "We go now. Stay low. Move fast. We find Lawoaka and the others, and we get the hell out."

The three of them slipped from the barge and into the shadows of Orcas Island.

The compound was eerily quiet at this hour. The faintest hint of dawn was just beginning to creep over the horizon, casting long shadows between the buildings. Graham led the way, navigating the maze of alleyways and abandoned structures that had become the terrorists' stronghold.

Mark moved beside him, scanning every dark corner. "Where do you think they're keeping them?"

Graham exhaled. "They always keep prisoners in the same place—centralized, guarded, but not too close to their own quarters. They don't want captives too close, in case they try to revolt."

McCann grunted. "So we head toward the middle of town."

Graham nodded. "It's this way. Not too far from the arena they set up."

They moved quickly, ducking behind cover whenever necessary. The streets were quiet, the few patrols lazy and unalert. That was their advantage—the routine, the lack of expectation.

The closer they got to the compound, the more oppressive the air became. Graham could feel the weight of the mission pressing down on him, heavier than the rifle in his hands. The thought of Lawoaka in enemy hands fueled him, pushing him forward.

They stopped at a fence wrapped in razor wire, its gate guarded by two men leaning against a rusted truck, sharing a cigarette. Their posture was relaxed, unconcerned.

Mark gestured toward them. "Easy pickings."

Graham nodded, signaling for McCann to circle left. He watched as McCann disappeared into the darkness, then glanced at Mark. "We take them quick and quiet."

Mark grinned. "That's the only way I work."

A moment later, a dull thud signaled McCann's attack. Graham moved instantly, crossing the short distance between him and the second guard, his blade slicing through flesh before the man could react.

Both bodies hit the ground, silent as ghosts.

Graham motioned for the others to move. The prison was close now. Inside, Lawoaka and the others were waiting.

And the sun was beginning to rise.

CHAPTER 11 - THE SILENT CRY

The prison smelled of damp rot and human despair. Graham pressed his back against the cold stone wall, breathing slow and steady, listening.

A single guard stood at the entrance, pacing lazily, his rifle slung over his shoulder. His posture was loose, unaware. This was routine for him. No one ever fought back here. Not on the island. No one ever escaped.

McCann moved first. Silent as a shadow, he crept behind the man, his knife flashing under the dim torchlight before sinking deep into his target's throat. The guard jerked, a gurgled sound caught in his throat, but McCann clamped a hand over his mouth and lowered him carefully to the ground.

Mark nodded to Graham. They were in.

The air inside was thick with the stench of sweat, filth, and sickness. The prison wasn't large—just a converted warehouse with rusted iron bars sectioning off different holding areas. Rows of women huddled on the cold floor, their faces gaunt, their eyes hollow. Some barely lifted their heads at the sound of boots approaching, while others flinched, pressing against the walls in fear.

Graham scanned their faces, searching. Where was Lawoaka?

Then he saw her.

She was thinner than he remembered, her once-vibrant brown skin pale with malnutrition. Her hair hung in tangled strands over her face, but her eyes—deep pools of sorrow—locked onto his.

Graham moved quickly, kneeling beside her, his fingers fumbling with the shackles around her wrists. "Lawoaka, we're getting you out."

She barely reacted. The other women stirred as Mark and McCann worked to free them, but Lawoaka didn't move. Instead, her hands gripped the edge of her torn garment, knuckles white with tension.

Graham touched her shoulder. "Lawoaka—"

She twisted away from him and stumbled toward the back of the cell. A small, reinforced door stood there, its rusted metal frame bolted shut.

Lawoaka pounded on it with her fists, a soundless cry breaking from her lips. Her shoulders heaved with emotion, but no words came.

McCann, still securing another woman's shackles, turned sharply. "What the hell is she doing?"

Graham was at her side in an instant. He pulled his knife

from its sheath and jammed it into the lock, but the rusted mechanism wouldn't give.

Lawoaka turned wild, her fingers clawing at the door, her breath coming in short, frantic bursts. Tears streaked her dirty face.

McCann muttered, "Jesus." He stepped up, gripping his knife, and wedged it into the rusted lock. With a hard jerk, the metal groaned. Another hit, and the door swung open.

Graham caught Lawoaka as she lunged inside.

And then—his breath caught.

Infants.

Tiny, swaddled bodies. Some crying softly, others eerily silent.

There were only three mothers who rushed forward, including Lawoaka, scooping up their babies as if their souls depended on it.

Graham's stomach twisted. Where were the rest?

He looked to McCann, whose hardened face betrayed nothing, but his grip on his rifle tightened.

"We don't have time for this," Mark hissed. "We need to move."

Graham forced his voice to stay steady. "Then let's go."

He turned back to Lawoaka, who was clutching her baby to her chest, rocking the child with desperate intensity. She still hadn't said a word.

Graham touched her arm gently. "We need to go now."

She lifted her gaze, and something in her expression shattered him.

She wasn't silent because of fear. She wasn't silent because of shock.

She physically couldn't speak.

McCann exhaled harshly, realization dawning. "They cut out her tongue."

Graham's hands clenched into fists.

He looked at the other women, many of them trembling, barely strong enough to walk. These women had survived hell, and now they had to escape it.

"Help them," he ordered.

Mark and McCann hoisted the weakest onto their feet, steadying them as they moved.

One of the women carried another child, pressing the baby against her body to keep it warm. Graham's gut churned. Three babies. Only three.

There had to be others. What had happened to them?

Graham forced his mind to focus. Later. They would figure that out later.

Right now, they had to get out.

The halls were eerily quiet as they made their way toward the dock. Too quiet.

Graham led the way, his heart pounding in his ears. Just get to the barge. Just get to the barge. Just get them out.

When they stepped outside, a thin mist had settled over the water, muting the light from the torches along the dock. Arlen was, waiting.

McCann and Mark helped the women across the gangplank, steadying their weakened bodies as they climbed aboard.

Graham turned back for one last sweep— and that's when he heard it.

The sharp clatter of boots on stone.

Shouting.

Then— gunfire.

A bullet pinged off the railing of the barge. Graham ducked, shoving Lawoaka down as she shielded her baby.

Mark raised his rifle, scanning the darkness. "How the hell did they know?"

Arlen, still at the helm, swore. "They must've realized the barge was leaving too early!"

More voices rose in the distance, barking in Arabic. They were coming. Fast.

Graham's mind raced. They weren't ready for a firefight.

They needed to leave. Now.

"Arlen!" Graham barked. "Get us out of here!"

The young man hesitated for only a second before throwing the throttle forward. The barge lurched further away from the dock.

Graham turned back, gripping his rifle. The guards were now in full sprint, their weapons raised.

"Mark, McCann—cover us!"

A burst of gunfire lit up the night. The guards dove for cover, bullets splintering wood and kicking up dust.

The barge moved too slowly—the heavy weight of bodies and cargo dragging against the current.

"Come on, come on," Graham muttered.

One of the women screamed as a bullet ricocheted off the railing.

McCann pulled her down, shielding her with his body. "We need to move faster, Arlen!"

"I'm trying!" Arlen gritted out, adjusting the controls.

The dock began to shrink in the distance, but the gunfire didn't stop. More guards appeared, their shouts growing fainter as the barge crept toward deeper water.

Almost there. Almost free.

Graham exhaled, his rifle still raised. His heart hammered in his chest.

They had made it off the island.

But they weren't safe yet.

And in the distance, silhouetted against the fading lights of Orcas Island— another boat was coming.

A boat that wasn't theirs.

CHAPTER 12 - THE PURSUIT ACROSS THE WATER

The sea stretched out like a vast, dark abyss around them, the night air thick with salt and tension. The stolen barge chugged forward, heavy and slow against the water. Graham stood at the stern, rifle in hand, his eyes locked on the approaching boat in the distance.

"How fast is it coming?" he asked, voice tight.

Arlen, gripping the wheel with white-knuckled hands, didn't look back. "Faster than us."

McCann, crouched near the railing, peered through the darkness. "It's a patrol boat. Smaller, lighter. Probably twenty knots at least."

Graham exhaled sharply. That meant the enemy had the advantage. They were coming—fast.

Behind them, trailing at a safe distance, Corey piloted the smaller boat with Tehya and Marcy aboard. If the patrol boat caught sight of them, it would be over.

Mark's voice was low. "They could have spotted us already."

Or they could just be responding to the gunfire from the docks. Either way, Graham couldn't take the chance.

"We need to find cover," he said.

"Where?" McCann asked. "We're in the middle of open water."

Graham turned to Arlen. "You've been watching this route. Where can we hide?"

Arlen's jaw clenched, his gaze scanning the shoreline. "There's a shallow cove up ahead. Rocky, tight, but the mist rolls in thick this time of night. If we kill the engine and sit still, they might pass us."

Might.

It wasn't much of a plan, but they didn't have a better one.

"Do it," Graham ordered. "Get us in there."

Arlen adjusted course, veering the barge toward the dark outline of land. The water here was cold, rough, the wind picking up and cutting through them like ice. Graham caught sight of Lawoaka, huddled in the shadows with the other women, clutching her baby to her chest.

Her expression was unreadable, but her fear was unmistakable.

They had to survive this.

Corey's Dilemma

Trailing behind in the small boat, Corey kept his grip

steady on the wheel, keeping a low profile in the darkness. Tehya and Marcy sat huddled near the stern, silent, watching.

"What the hell is Dad doing?" Tehya whispered, her breath visible in the cold air.

"He's making a move," Corey muttered.

"But where?" Marcy asked. "They're going toward the coast."

Corey narrowed his eyes. "He's trying to disappear."

"But what about us?" Tehya pressed.

"We stick to the plan," Corey said, keeping the boat just far enough back. "If things go south, we get out."

He glanced at Tehya, knowing she hated those words.

She wanted to be in the fight. She always had. But Graham had made it clear—her job was survival.

Still, Corey could feel it in his gut. Something was about to go wrong.

The Trap in the Cove

The mist thickened as they neared the cove, shrouding the barge in swirling gray.

"Kill the engine," Graham ordered.

Arlen pulled the throttle back. The low hum of the motor faded into nothing. The barge drifted, the weight of its stolen cargo keeping it moving just enough to settle into the natural pull of the water.

The patrol boat's engine roared louder, slicing through the night.

McCann crouched lower, his rifle ready. "If they pass us, we let them go. If they slow down…"

Graham didn't need him to finish.

If the enemy slowed, they'd have no choice but to fight.

The women aboard held their breath, every one of them rigid with fear. Lawoaka's baby stirred, but she held the child tightly, rocking gently, willing it into silence.

Then the enemy boat came into view.

Graham gritted his teeth.

It was closer than expected.

The sleek black hull cut through the water with ease, spotlights flicking back and forth across the surface.

"Hold," Graham murmured.

They waited.

The light swept over the water—closer, closer—then passed over the barge.

No reaction.

Graham stilled. His heart pounded.

The light didn't come back.

The boat kept moving.

It was passing them.

For a long, tense moment, Graham didn't move, didn't breathe.

Then McCann whispered, "Holy shit."

Graham finally let out a slow breath.

"They didn't see us," Mark muttered.

Or they weren't looking for them.

Not yet.

An Unwelcome Visitor

They waited in silence for five minutes. Ten.

Then Arlen, still gripping the controls, exhaled. "We're clear."

Graham wasn't convinced. "Not yet."

Then—a new sound.

A second set of engines. Slower, heavier.

Graham's stomach dropped.

"They sent a second patrol," McCann whispered. "Shit."

The new boat was closer than the first.

And it was turning toward them.

"Move," Graham snapped. "Now."

Arlen threw the throttle forward. The barge lurched, the engine roaring back to life.

The second patrol boat had slowed, its spotlight locked on them. The radio crackled again, the voice sharp, angry, demanding in Arabic.

Arlen looked to Graham, waiting for an order.

Graham grabbed the radio before Arlen could hesitate. His voice was ice-cold, unwavering.

"You're too late," he said, his tone flat, authoritative. "The barge is ours. The prisoners are ours. And if you want to die tonight, you're welcome to try and take it back."

The radio went silent.

McCann smirked. "Well, that oughta get their attention."

Mark exhaled sharply, shifting his grip on his rifle. "Hope you know what you're doing."

Graham kept his gaze locked on the patrol boat, waiting.

The radio crackled again, but this time, the voice wasn't yelling. It was hushed, uncertain. Then, suddenly—the engine of the patrol boat roared to life.

They were pulling back.

Arlen let out a breath. "Damn. You just called their bluff."

"They're not used to someone standing up to them," Graham muttered, setting the radio down. "Now they have to decide if it's worth coming after us."

"Will they?" McCann asked.

Graham gritted his teeth, watching the retreating boat, its lights dimming as it turned back toward the island.

"Maybe not tonight," he said. "But they will."

Silence stretched between them.

Then Arlen chuckled under his breath. "Damn, Graham. I was just gonna tell them to take a hike."

McCann shook his head. "Yeah, well, Graham just declared war."

Graham picked up his rifle again. "It been war. You're just too young to remember what it was like before."

The second patrol boat turned away.

Graham could hardly believe it.

They were clear.

For now.

CHAPTER 13 - MIDNIGHT WATERS

The night still cloaked the Puget Sound, but the unease in Graham's gut said it wouldn't protect them much longer. They'd gotten off the island, stolen the barge, and rescued the prisoners. Too easy. He never believed for a second that they were in the clear.

Graham stood at the stern, watching the dark waters churn behind them, the heavy weight of the barge cutting sluggishly through the waves. Something wasn't right. It wasn't just paranoia this time.

That's when he saw Tehya, gripping the rail of Corey's boat, eyes locked on the horizon.

"Dad!" she shouted across the water, voice sharp, urgent. "I see something—"

A flash of light.

Then another.

Graham snatched the binoculars from McCann, raising them to his eyes.

A second boat. Bigger. Faster. And armed.

Graham's stomach dropped as the moonlight glinted off something metallic, mounted at the bow.

"A machine gun," Arlen muttered beside him, his voice grim. "Damn it. They sent a gunboat."

The air turned colder around them, the realization sinking in. The terrorists had sent backup.

They weren't just pursuing. They were hunting.

The Plan to Divide

Graham lowered the binoculars, already calculating their next move. "We can't outrun them. Not in this tin bucket.

McCann cursed under his breath. "We're sitting ducks on this thing."

Arlen grabbed Graham's arm, urgency flickering in his eyes. "We need to split up. Break the pattern. They won't know who to chase."

Graham turned sharply to face him. "You got something in mind?"

Arlen nodded. "There's a cove past the next channel. We ditch the barge. Take smaller boats. We scatter."

"That's insane." Mark shook his head. "We'll be too exposed."

"We're already exposed," Arlen shot back. "They'll hit this

thing with everything they've got once they're close enough. But if we break into smaller groups, they can't chase all of us."

Graham exhaled sharply, his mind already racing through the logistics. Thirty prisoners. Three infants. Not enough supplies. But Arlen was right. The barge was too slow, too big. They'd never make it to safety like this.

He nodded, making the call.

"All right. We split into three groups."

He pointed at Corey's boat, where Tehya and Marcy were already waiting.

"Corey takes Tehya, Marcy, and ten prisoners. They'll go north, loop toward the coast. If they hug the shoreline, they can stay hidden."

Corey nodded once, eyes sharp. "We'll handle it."

Graham turned to Mark and McCann. "You two take another group. Head east. Stick to the shadows, keep quiet."

Mark's jaw tensed. "And you?"

"I take Arlen and the last ten," Graham said. "We go west. Deeper into the Sound."

McCann gave him a long, unreadable look. "You sure about this?"

Graham's grip tightened on his rifle. "We don't have a choice."

The Split

They worked fast.

The prisoners whispered in panicked voices, their fear only barely contained. Some were too weak to argue. The mothers held their babies close, clutching them with shaking hands.

Graham and Arlen helped them into the boats, dividing the group as efficiently as possible.

Tehya lingered near Graham, arms crossed, watching him carefully.

"You're really doing this," she said, not quite a question.

He met her gaze. "It's the only way."

Tehya hesitated, then nodded once. "I'll see you on the other side."

Graham gripped her shoulder, squeezing just for a second. Then he let go.

Corey gunned the engine softly, steering away from the barge. One boat down.

Mark and McCann were next, leading their group toward the eastern inlet, disappearing into the darkness.

Graham and Arlen stayed last, watching the barge drift. Graham felt a pang of finality as he let it go, the vessel they had fought for now abandoned to the tide.

Then, the gunboat rounded the bend.

"Go," Arlen hissed.

Graham shoved the throttle forward. Their boat surged into the darkness.

Pursuit in the Night

They could hear it first. The deep, growling hum of a diesel engine, the slap of water against the hull. The terrorists were coming fast.

Graham didn't look back. Didn't need to. He knew they were hunting them now.

Arlen cursed under his breath. "I think they're following us."

Graham kept his voice steady. "Good."

Arlen gave him a sharp look. "Good?"

Graham finally looked back. The gunboat was closing the gap, its bow slicing through the water like a shark on the hunt.

"They don't know the others split off," Graham said. "That means they're coming for us."

Arlen's expression shifted. Understanding. Then resolve.

"We lead them away."

Graham nodded. "We lead them away."

The gunboat's spotlight swung across the water, catching the edge of their wake.

A voice shouted in Arabic.

Then—

The first bullet cracked past them.

Arlen jerked the wheel, the boat veering hard as the gunfire ripped across the surface of the water.

Graham gritted his teeth, raising his rifle, but it was too dark, too rough.

They needed cover.

They needed a way out.

And fast.

CHAPTER 14 - LOST IN THE SOUND

The wind cut like a blade across the waves, the salt spray mixing with the acrid scent of fuel and blood. The boat lurched violently, the engine sputtering, barely keeping them ahead of the gunboat on their tail.

Bullets zipped past them, punching through the wooden hull, sending sharp splinters flying. Graham hunched low, gripping the side of the boat as another burst of automatic fire rattled into the night.

They weren't going to make it.

Not unless Arlen's plan worked.

"Arlen, tell me you still know these waters!" Graham shouted over the roar of the wind and crashing waves.

Arlen's hands were tight on the wheel, eyes locked ahead. "I know them better than they do."

"That's not saying much!"

Arlen flashed a tense grin before banking the boat hard to

the left. The hull groaned in protest as it nearly tipped. The prisoners screamed, clutching onto whatever they could.

"Hold on!" Arlen barked.

Graham threw his weight to the opposite side to balance them as they rocketed toward the black maw of the inlet.

The gunboat followed. Faster. Heavier. Armed to the teeth.

"They're gonna ram us!" a woman shouted from the stern, her face pale in the moonlight.

Graham could see it too. The gunboat was closing fast, angling for a hit that would send them spinning into the rocks.

Arlen didn't flinch.

Instead, he waited.

Waited too long.

Then—

A sharp turn.

The boat lurched.

Graham grabbed onto the rail as they narrowly missed the jagged teeth of a rock outcropping—a hidden reef that had claimed boats before.

The gunboat wasn't so lucky.

A sickening crunch.

The impact ripped through the night, the gunboat slamming full-speed into the rocks.

Graham saw men thrown overboard, heard shouts of panic, saw the wreckage bloom into a fireball as the fuel tank ruptured.

And then—silence.

Only the wind, the slapping of the waves against the ruined vessel.

They'd done it.

Graham exhaled, chest heaving. "That was stupid."

Arlen, grinning wildly, wiped sweat from his brow. "Yeah. But it worked."

Graham clapped him on the shoulder, but his relief was short-lived.

Water was pooling at their feet.

Arlen cursed as he looked down. "The hull's hit bad. We're taking on water."

Graham's relief vanished.

They weren't out of this yet.

"The engine?" Graham asked, his stomach sinking.

Arlen gave it a grim look. "Running on fumes."

No radio. No backup. No one knew where they were.

Graham turned toward the huddled prisoners, fear in their eyes. The injured woman wasn't moving anymore.

"She's gone," a prisoner muttered.

No one spoke.

The waves rocked them hard, the boat struggling under its own weight.

"Land," Arlen said, scanning the horizon. "We need land."

Graham nodded, casting one last look at the stars above.

Then—

The boat lurched.

The water rushed in.

And everything went dark.

CHAPTER 15 - NO WORD FROM GRAHAM

The sun crept over the horizon, a weak sliver of light stretching across the waters of Deception Pass. The boat rocked beneath Tehya as she stood at the bow, scanning the water for any sign of her father.

Nothing.

Just endless rippling waves, the foam curling in the dim morning glow. The air smelled of salt and damp wood, and the cold gnawed at her fingers, making them stiff against the railing.

She hugged herself. Graham should be here by now.

Corey pulled the boat in tight against the dock, guiding it with practiced ease. Marcy clutched onto the edge of the boat, her face pale with exhaustion, but she was silent, lost in her own thoughts.

Ten prisoners sat huddled together, wrapped in whatever spare blankets and jackets they'd scrounged from the barge.

Women, tired and battered, but free. Some clung to each other, whispering quietly in languages Tehya didn't understand. Others stared blankly ahead, as if their minds hadn't caught up to the fact that they were no longer captives.

Corey cut the engine, letting the boat drift the last few feet before he hopped onto the dock. "All right," he called out, rubbing his hands together. "Let's get everyone off."

The prisoners moved slowly, their bodies stiff from the cold and the long ride.

Tehya barely noticed. Her eyes were still on the water.

Where was he?

Mark and McCann's boat was just now pulling in, their figures moving as they guided their own group of freed women ashore. McCann was the first to hop down onto the dock, steadying the boat as Mark helped the last woman off.

Tehya stepped forward immediately. "Where's Dad?"

McCann shook his head. "Haven't seen him."

Tehya's stomach dropped. "What do you mean?"

Mark met her eyes, his own face tight with exhaustion. "We split up, Tehya. Three boats. We made it here. They... they haven't yet."

The words hit her like a fist to the gut.

She turned back toward the water, her hands gripping the wooden railing so hard her knuckles turned white. The waves rolled, black and endless, stretching toward the distant horizon.

Graham's boat should have been right behind them.

"They could be out there, lost," she whispered.

Corey set a hand on her shoulder. "They'll show up soon."

But his voice didn't sound sure.

Tehya looked up at him, searching his face for the certainty she needed. "You don't know that."

Corey sighed, running a hand through his wind-tangled hair. "No, I don't. But your dad's been through worse. If anyone can make it back, it's him."

Tehya nodded slowly, but her gut still twisted.

She turned back to the waves. She couldn't just stand here. She needed to do something.

"I want to go look for them," she said suddenly.

Corey's hand tightened on her shoulder. "No way."

Tehya spun on him, angry now. "Why not? We have a boat. We—"

"We have twenty people who need shelter," Corey cut in, his tone firm. "And let's not forget—when we left here last, someone was shooting at us. We can't just go cruising around in open water looking for trouble."

Tehya gritted her teeth. "We can't just leave them out there."

"We're not," Mark interrupted, stepping up beside Corey. "We're gonna wait. Give them time. They might already be heading in from another direction."

Tehya clenched her fists. It wasn't enough.

But she knew they were right.

She inhaled deeply, forcing herself to push down the panic clawing at her chest.

Corey softened his tone. "Listen, Tehya. We get these people to safety first. Then we figure out a plan. Your dad would want that."

Her throat tightened. He was right. Graham would put the mission first.

But she wasn't Graham.

She looked back at the empty, endless water. The sun was climbing higher, streaking the sky with hints of soft pink and gold. It should've been a beautiful sight.

Instead, it felt like a warning.

Graham was still out there. Somewhere.

And Tehya had a terrible feeling they were running out of time.

CHAPTER 16 - THE WAITING GAME

The wind howled through the trees, a ghostly moan that rattled the tent walls around her. Clarisse sat at the radio station, staring at the lifeless receiver, willing it to crackle with sound. The embers of the fire in the hearth behind her pulsed softly, casting long shadows along the wooden walls, but the warmth did nothing to settle the cold that had seeped into her chest.

Graham was supposed to have checked in by now.

Instead, the radio had been silent for hours.

Paige shifted in the chair beside her, arms wrapped around her midsection, her fingers absently rubbing the small swell of her belly. She didn't say anything, but she didn't have to—Clarisse could feel her unease like a second heartbeat in the room.

Across from them, Sam stood near the entrance, arms crossed, face grim. He hadn't spoken much since Graham left, but now, as the silence stretched on, his fingers drummed impatiently against his bicep.

Then—

A sharp burst of static.

Clarisse bolted upright, grabbing the receiver. The frequency wavered, but then a familiar voice cut through.

"Cascade, this is McCann. We're coming in. Expect company."

Clarisse inhaled sharply. She pressed down on the button. "Copy that, McCann. Report."

"We've got thirty prisoners with us and three infants." His voice was steady but clipped. "All women. Some injured but mobile."

Paige let out a slow breath. Thirty.

Clarisse felt her heart kick against her ribs. That was a large number to shelter, but they'd manage.

Then she registered what McCann hadn't said.

Her grip tightened on the radio. "And Graham?"

The pause on the other end was too long.

"Not with us."

Clarisse closed her eyes. Damn it, Graham.

Sam muttered a curse under his breath. Paige sat up straighter, her lips pressing into a thin line.

Clarisse forced herself to stay calm. "Where was he last seen?"

More static. Then McCann's voice again.

"Last we saw, he was headed inland with his group. We had to split up. No radio contact since. It's a lot to explain."

Clarisse swallowed, pushing away the worst thoughts.

That didn't mean anything. Maybe Graham had run into trouble, but he was resourceful. He would have found a way.

She needed more information.

"McCann, who's with him?"

McCann hesitated. "Can't say over radio. But he's not alone."

Clarisse exhaled through her nose, forcing herself to stay steady. If McCann was avoiding specifics, it meant something had gone wrong—but they were still being cautious about what they revealed.

Clarisse glanced at Sam, who was watching her with an unreadable expression. He had to be thinking the same thing.

The radio crackled again, and this time, a different voice came through.

Corey.

"Clarisse."

Her stomach tightened. "I'm here."

The way Corey said her name—low, careful—sent a chill down her spine.

"We're all okay," he said first, like he knew that's what she needed to hear. "The prisoners are safe, and we're helping them get settled. But... we haven't seen Graham."

Clarisse's pulse kicked faster.

She ignored the way Sam's eyes flicked to her. Ignored the way Paige sat perfectly still, waiting for her reaction.

"Are you saying you think he's not coming back?"

Corey hesitated.

Then, his voice lowered, quieter now.

"I'm saying... it's been a long time."

Clarisse clenched her jaw. "He's survived worse."

Corey exhaled through the receiver. "I know."

She didn't like the way he said that.

Didn't like the doubt in his voice.

Didn't like how it made her stomach twist.

A long pause stretched between them.

Finally, Corey spoke again, voice softer. "How are you holding up?"

Clarisse closed her eyes. Damn him for asking.

"Fine," she said flatly.

Another pause.

"You always say that," Corey murmured.

Her fingers tightened around the receiver.

She didn't have time for this. For whatever this was.

But Corey had always had a way of getting under her skin.

Of making her feel things she didn't want to feel.

She cleared her throat, pushing past it. "How soon can you move the prisoners?"

"McCann and Mark are already working on it," Corey said, easily shifting gears. "We need a plan before we head inland."

"You'll have a plan," Clarisse assured him. "We'll be ready."

Corey didn't answer right away.

Then, so quietly she almost missed it:

"Clarisse."

She waited.

"Be careful."

Her chest tightened.

Her voice was steady when she replied. "You, too."

And then the radio went silent.

Clarisse set the receiver down slowly, staring at it for a long moment before looking up.

Paige's eyes were dark with worry. Sam was still watching her, arms crossed.

And deep in her gut, a slow, creeping fear began to take hold.

CHAPTER 17 - THE STRANGER IN THE WOODS

Corey crouched beside the bullet-riddled truck, running his fingers along the ragged edge of a hole in the hood. The cold metal sent a shiver through him, but it wasn't the wind cutting through his jacket that made him uneasy. The truck was done for. No gas, shot-up tires, engine probably useless. Even if they had a miracle mechanic in their midst, there was no salvaging it—not when they had twenty freezing prisoners, two infants, and no way to transport them.

Mark McCann stood beside him, arms crossed, expression dark. "It's worse than I thought," he muttered.

Corey exhaled, straightening. "Yeah."

McCann adjusted the rifle slung over his chest, his gaze flicking toward the tree line. "And I don't like how quiet it is."

Corey followed his line of sight. The forest stretched out

beyond them, dark and thick, the shadows between the trees deepening as the sun rose from the horizon. The wind rustled the branches, and the distant cry of a gull echoed over the water, but there was something... off. No small animal scurrying. No birds in the underbrush.

The silence wasn't natural. It felt like the world was waiting.

He turned his attention to Tehya. She stood near the shore, her arms wrapped around herself, staring across the water. The last time she'd seen her father, he was stepping onto that boat, drawing the gun boat out to sea with Arlen and the rest. He had promised her he'd return. But promises didn't mean much these days.

Corey wanted to say something—anything—to reassure her, but what good would empty words do?

Instead, he focused on the problem at hand. The truck. The stranded people. The need for shelter before night fell.

McCann's posture shifted. He wasn't looking at Tehya anymore. His head turned slightly, eyes narrowing as his shoulders tensed. Corey knew that look.

Something was coming.

Corey didn't hesitate—his rifle was in his hands before he even registered movement. He scanned the tree line, following McCann's lead, finger light on the trigger.

Then, movement. A figure stumbled out of the woods.

"Hands where I can see 'em!" McCann barked, stepping forward, his rifle raised.

The man—tall, wiry, and unkempt—froze. His hands lifted in a lazy, slow motion, palms out. He had a wild look to him, hair hanging in tangled ropes around his face, his eyes glassy. His clothes were layered—patched, ragged, but not filthy.

McCann took another step. "Who the hell are you?"

The man grinned, teeth white in the gloom. "Whoa, easy there, soldier," he drawled, his voice thick with something—weed, maybe, or something stronger.

Corey tightened his grip on his rifle.

McCann didn't lower his gun. "I said—who are you?"

The man rocked slightly on his heels. "Name's Flint." He gave a lazy half-bow. "And before you go shootin' me, I come in peace. And, uh..." He squinted at the bullet-riddled truck. "Looks like y'all might need a ride."

McCann's rifle didn't waver. "How the hell do you know that?"

Flint chuckled, rubbing his chin as if considering his words. "Well, let's just say... word travels. The folks on the radio? They heard about what happened here. Figured you might be in a tight spot." He grinned. "So, they sent me."

Corey exchanged a look with McCann.

McCann scowled. "With what?"

Flint's grin stretched wider. "A bus."

Corey stared at him. "A *bus*?"

"Big, yellow, and a little worse for wear, but she runs." Flint dropped his hands, but McCann's rifle stayed on him. He didn't seem to care. "Look, man, I get it. You don't trust me. Hell, I don't trust *you* either."

McCann's jaw tightened. "Then why are you here?"

Flint sighed dramatically. "Because life's all about chances, man. You take 'em, or you don't."

Corey stepped forward. "And if we don't?"

Flint shrugged. "Then I go back, tell 'em you turned it down, and you figure something else out." He spread his arms. "Simple as that."

McCann looked back at Corey. "This smells wrong."

Corey nodded. "Yeah."

Flint exhaled sharply. "Look, I get it. You think maybe *we* were the ones who did this." He gestured to the bullet-ridden truck. "Maybe you think this is a setup, that I'm luring you into some kinda trap."

McCann didn't move.

Flint smirked. "But let's be real, man. If it *was* a trap, you'd already be dead."

The words hung in the air.

Corey's grip on his rifle tightened. He hated how logical that was.

Tehya turned from the water, finally speaking. "We should take the chance."

Corey looked at her.

She met his gaze, steady. "We don't have another option."

McCann exhaled through his nose, then turned back to Flint. "Where's the bus?"

Flint's grin returned. "Just up the road. About a mile."

McCann gave Corey a look, then muttered, "We're checking it out first."

Corey nodded.

McCann turned to Mark and Marcy, who had been

standing back with the others. "Keep everyone here, weapons ready. If we're not back in an hour..." He didn't finish.

Mark understood.

Flint waved a hand. "C'mon then, gentlemen. Let's go for a little walk."

The Walk to the Bus

Flint moved like a man who had nowhere important to be. Corey and McCann kept a few paces behind him, watching his every step.

"So," Flint drawled as they walked. "What's your deal, huh? You military or something?"

McCann didn't answer.

Flint grinned. "Tight-lipped. I like that."

They moved through the trees, the road up ahead cracked and covered in moss. There hadn't been working infrastructure in a long time, but it was clear this area had been traveled recently.

"You got kids back there?" Flint asked after a moment.

Corey stiffened.

Flint glanced back, his expression less amused. "Heard someone mention prisoners over the radio." He shrugged. "Lot of people out here don't make it."

McCann's rifle twitched slightly.

Flint lifted his hands again. "Relax. *I'm* not saying anything you don't know. Just saying... people get desperate."

Corey swallowed hard. He knew that better than anyone.

Finally, they reached the crest of a hill, and Flint gestured forward. "Ta-da."

The bus sat on the side of the road, faded yellow with *Cascade School District* still faintly visible under years of grime. It was rough—patched windows, missing side panels, but it *looked* like it could move.

McCann and Corey exchanged a glance.

Flint leaned against a tree. "So?"

McCann exhaled. "We check it first."

"I'll go. You keep him here," Corey growled as scanned the area for a trap.

McCann held the barrel end of his gun in Flint's general direction as Corey climbed inside. The seats were torn up, some missing entirely, but it wasn't the worst condition he'd seen.

Then he turned the key.

The bus rumbled to life.

His stomach clenched. They *had* to take the chance.

McCann still looked skeptical.

Flint grinned. "Guess it's decision time."

McCann sighed. Then, finally, he muttered, "Let's get everyone loaded up."

Flint's grin widened. "Smart move, soldier."

Corey just hoped it wasn't a mistake as he drove the bus closer to pick up the group.

When Flint caught up, he took one last drag from his cigarette, then flicked it into the dirt, grinding it under his boot. "Well, guess my job's done here," he muttered, shouldering his worn-out backpack.

McCann narrowed his eyes. "You're not coming with us?"

Flint snorted. "Hell no, man. Bellingham's where I belong. Y'all got your mission, I got mine." He gave them a lazy salute. "Good luck with your lost captain. Hope he's not fish food."

Corey clenched his jaw, watching as Flint ambled off into the trees, disappearing into the darkness like a ghost. There was something about the guy that felt like bad luck trailing in his wake, but at least he had come through with the bus.

McCann exhaled through his nose, then turned back to Mark, who had already climbed into the driver's seat. "Get them back to camp. Fast."

Mark gave a short nod, then reached for the key in the ignition. The bus rattled to life again, coughing up thick smoke as the engine sputtered to a low rumble.

Inside, Marcy was moving through the rows, checking on the women, while McCann stood near the door, scanning the tree line one last time.

Corey turned toward Tehya, who still stood stiffly near the shore, arms wrapped tightly around herself.

"You're coming," Corey told her.

She shook her head. "No. I'll wait."

Corey tightened his grip on the rifle slung across his chest. "Not happening. You're not staying out here alone."

Tehya's eyes burned into his. "And if they call in while we're gone? If Graham—if my dad—" Her voice cracked, and she swallowed hard. "I can't risk missing him."

Corey's stomach twisted. He understood. He hated that he understood.

"We're coming back," McCann said, his voice firm as he stepped down from the bus. "As soon as we get them settled, we'll be back out here before sunrise."

Tehya didn't move.

Corey hesitated, then nodded. "I'll stay with her."

McCann's jaw tensed, but he didn't argue. He knew Tehya wasn't leaving, and there was no way in hell they were leaving her alone.

Mark pulled the door shut with a metallic groan, the engine revving as he eased the bus onto the road. The prisoners huddled together inside, Marcy tending to one of the infants, McCann taking up a position near the front.

The bus lurched forward, grinding against the pavement as it disappeared into the darkness, leaving Corey and Tehya alone on the desolate stretch of road.

The wind howled off the water, biting through Corey's jacket. He rolled his shoulders and glanced at Tehya, who had turned back toward the water, staring into the black waves like they might give her an answer.

He sighed. It was going to be a long day.

Half an hour later, the static crackled through the radio before Clarisse's voice came through, tinny but clear.

"Say again, Corey. The bus is on its way?"

Corey adjusted the frequency, shielding the radio from the biting wind with his hand. He turned his back to Tehya, who remained near the water's edge, her silhouette barely moving against the faint glow of the horizon.

"Yeah," he answered, keeping his voice low. "Mark's driving. McCann and Marcy are tending to the women. It's gonna take them over an hour to reach you, but they should be in before late afternoon."

Clarisse exhaled on the other end. "That's good news. We'll be ready for them. We're still scrambling for supplies."

Corey hesitated. "Listen… Tehya and I are staying behind."

Silence.

Then, "You mean Tehya refused to leave."

Corey's jaw tightened. "Yeah."

Clarisse sighed. "And you're humoring her?"

Corey rubbed his forehead. He glanced back at Tehya. She hadn't moved an inch, arms wrapped around herself, staring at the water like she could will her father's boat to appear from the void.

"There's no radio on Graham's boat," he reminded Clarisse. "We don't know if they had enough fuel. We don't know how far they made it. And if they're alive, we don't know which direction they'll come from."

"Exactly." Clarisse's voice was sharp but measured. "Corey, you and I both know he could come in by land, in a week, for all we know."

Corey clenched his teeth, eyes drifting back to Tehya's unmoving form. The weight of the truth settled heavy in his chest.

She was holding onto something fragile, something thin

as a thread, and if he snapped it too soon, he wasn't sure what would happen.

Clarisse's voice softened. "How long do you intend to humor her?"

Corey exhaled through his nose. "One day," he said finally. "I'll give her one day. Then I'll bring her home. No matter what."

Silence stretched between them.

"All right," Clarisse said at last. "One day."

The radio fell quiet.

Corey ran a hand down his face and turned toward the shore, toward Tehya, toward the waiting.

CHAPTER 18 - THE STORM ROLLS IN

Clarisse tightened the strap of her jacket as the first raindrops spattered against her shoulders. The cold wind had picked up in the last hour, rattling the loose canvas of the medical tent behind her. She barely noticed.

The radio crackled in her grip.

"We're close," McCann's voice came through, tight and clipped. "Another five minutes. The bus is... it's bad, Clarisse. I've seen worse, but not by much."

Clarisse's gut twisted. "How bad?"

"The women are in rough shape—exhausted, dehydrated, some injured. But it's the infants I'm worried about. One of them... I don't know if she's gonna make it."

Damn it. Clarisse pressed a hand to her forehead, forcing herself to think.

"All right. We'll be ready." She turned, scanning the camp. "Elara! Macy! Sam! Move!"

Sam stood near the central firepit, his rifle slung over his shoulder. He didn't move. The look he shot her was unreadable, but his hesitation was clear.

Clarisse stormed toward him. "Don't just stand there! Get the med tent ready! We need heat, blankets, food, water—"

Sam crossed his arms. "You sure about this?"

Clarisse's breath hitched, her pulse hammering in her ears. "What the hell do you mean?"

Sam's jaw tightened. "I mean, how many mouths can we feed, Clarisse? How many more can we afford to take in? We don't even know these people."

A crack of thunder rolled over the hills. Clarisse clenched her fists. "I don't give a damn if we know them. They needed rescuing. We rescued them. That means they're ours now."

Sam's lips pressed into a hard line, but he said nothing. He turned sharply and strode toward the med tent. Elara gave Clarisse a worried glance before hurrying after him.

Clarisse exhaled sharply. No time for that now.

The bus was coming.

The headlights were barely more than a dull glow in the fog and rain. Clarisse stood at the edge of camp, squinting into the distance as the rumbling growl of the engine grew louder, coughing and sputtering as if the damn thing might give out before making it up the last hill.

Then, finally, the yellow hulk emerged through the trees, its tires sloshing through mud as it pulled into camp. The brakes let out a horrible screech before the whole vehicle lurched to a stop.

The doors swung open.

Marcy was the first off, stepping down quickly before reaching up to help a frail woman descend. Mark was behind her, his expression tight, shoulders tense.

Clarisse saw it before she even heard the words.

Marcy snapped. "Can you give me some damn space, Mark?!"

Mark's hands curled into fists at his sides. He shook his head, muttering something, before stepping back.

Clarisse *almost* cared. She made a mental note of it. But right now? Not important.

Instead, she turned her attention to the women.

They came off the bus in pairs or in stumbling singles. Their clothes were torn, their faces gaunt. Some had fresh wounds, bruises, cracked lips. A few of them clutched each other for support. Others looked too exhausted to even notice the cold rain beginning to fall.

Marcy moved through them with quiet determination, offering hands, murmuring reassurances.

McCann came last, stepping out with the smallest bundle Clarisse had ever seen.

Her stomach clenched.

McCann didn't even look at her. He just strode past, straight toward the medical tent.

Clarisse followed.

Inside, the med tent was chaos.

Elara was already working, grabbing blankets, ushering women into cots, checking wounds and vitals.

Sam—despite his earlier doubts—was helping too, guiding a particularly weak woman to sit, handing out water.

Clarisse scanned the tent. "Where's Paige?"

Macy looked up from where she was helping remove wet coats from one of the women. "In the radio tent."

Clarisse nodded grimly. Of course.

Paige, like Tehya, was waiting.

Then McCann's voice cut through everything.

"Shit—Clarisse! We're losing her!"

Clarisse turned just in time to see McCann kneeling on the ground, cradling the tiny infant in his arms. The baby's skin had gone gray, her lips dark, her chest too still.

The room froze.

The storm outside howled, wind battering the tent's fabric, as Clarisse lunged forward.

Everything else could wait.

CHAPTER 19 - THE FIRE WITHIN

The rain came down in cold sheets, drumming against the bullet-riddled truck like a heartbeat. The fire Corey had started outside had been strong at first, burning hot with pine and driftwood, but the storm had smothered it, leaving only the damp scent of smoke clinging to the air.

Now, the only warmth they had was inside the truck, sheltered from the worst of the downpour. It was stripped bare—no seats, no dashboard, just a rusted-out husk that barely kept the wind from cutting through them.

But it was something.

Tehya pulled her knees up to her chest, her fingers numb as she plucked a piece of squirrel meat from the makeshift spit Corey had rigged with an old metal rod. The meat was tough, gamey, and tasted more like burned pine than anything remotely edible, but she chewed anyway.

Corey sat across from her, leaning against the truck's cold metal interior. His face was shadowed, the dim glow of the embers outside casting flickering light over his jawline.

He took a bite of his own, grimaced. "I think I overcooked it."

Tehya huffed a quiet laugh. "You think?"

Corey smirked but didn't reply. Instead, he studied her, his gaze unreadable as he chewed, then wiped his fingers against his jeans.

She looked away first.

Outside, the storm howled. Wind rushed through the shattered windshield, whistling through the gaping holes in the truck like ghosts whispering in the dark.

She hugged her arms tighter around herself.

Corey shifted. "You're thinking about him."

Tehya didn't answer.

Corey sighed. He set down his half-eaten squirrel leg and leaned forward, forearms resting on his knees. "Tehya…"

She swallowed hard. "He promised."

Corey didn't speak. He just watched her.

She clenched her jaw. "He said he'd come back. He—" Her voice wavered. She hated how weak she sounded.

Corey's expression didn't change.

Tehya let out a slow breath, pressing her hands to her face. "I know it was the right thing to do. I know why he did it. But, Corey, he left me before."

Her voice broke on the last word, shame rising in her throat.

She expected Corey to dismiss it, to tell her she was being stupid, that she knew better.

But he didn't.

Instead, he reached across the space between them, his hand warm as it closed over hers.

"You think he abandoned you back then," Corey said, his voice steady, "but you know that's not what happened."

Tehya shook her head, pulling her hand free. "You don't get it."

Corey didn't move. "I do."

She looked at him sharply, ready to argue, but something in his dark eyes stopped her.

He did understand.

Corey was the only one who'd ever seen it—the way she held onto that bitterness, the fear that maybe, deep down, she really hadn't been enough to keep Graham from leaving.

"I hated him," she whispered. "I hated him for so long."

Corey nodded, waiting.

Her throat tightened. "And now he's—" She choked on the words, unable to finish.

She didn't want to say it.

Didn't want to admit that the possibility of her father being gone forever felt like it was ripping her apart from the inside out.

Corey moved closer, the warmth of him replacing the cold creeping into her bones. "Tehya, your dad didn't leave you back then, and he sure as hell isn't leaving you now."

Tears pricked at her eyes, hot and unwanted.

Corey's voice softened. "He did what he had to do. Just like now."

She clenched her jaw. "I didn't ask him to."

Corey let out a slow breath. "Doesn't matter."

Tehya looked away, biting her lip.

Corey leaned his head back against the metal. "Look, I don't know what's happening out there. Maybe he's hurt. Maybe he's lost." He paused, his voice low. "Or maybe he's fighting like hell to get back to you."

The words hit her like a blow.

Because deep down, she knew.

Knew that Graham wouldn't have stayed away if he had a choice.

Knew that he'd risk everything—his life, his future, whatever safety he had—just to keep her safe.

And what had she done in return?

She'd spent half her life resenting him for a choice he never had.

Tears slipped down her cheek before she could stop them.

She hated crying.

Hated feeling this weak, this exposed.

But Corey didn't say anything.

He just sat there.

Letting her fall apart in the silence.

The rain pounded against the truck. The wind rattled the rusted frame. The world outside felt like it was ending.

But here, inside this broken shell of a vehicle, with the last warmth of the fire outside fading into darkness—

She wasn't alone.

And neither was Graham.

Wherever he was, he was fighting his way home.

Whether she liked it or not.

CHAPTER 20 - THE COST OF HOPE

The moment the bus lurched to a stop in the muddy clearing of Graham's camp, Clarisse was already moving.

"Get those doors open!" she barked, motioning to Sam and Elara, who scrambled forward, their boots sinking into the wet ground as rain pelted down around them. The weather had turned sour just, as if the sky itself understood the sheer weight of what was happening.

The air smelled of damp earth, exhaust fumes, and the unmistakable scent of sickness and exhaustion from the women and infants being transported.

McCann yelled again, his expression grim. "Clarisse," he called, hoisting a bundled infant against his chest. "This one's bad. Real bad."

Clarisse's stomach clenched as she ran toward him. "Bring the baby inside, now!"

McCann didn't hesitate. Behind him, Marcy was helping other women off the steps, but even as she offered a steadying hand, she turned her head toward Mark, snapping again something under her breath.

Clarisse caught the tail end of it—something about reckless driving—but there was no time to deal with it now.

"Move, move!" she urged, ushering the survivors toward the medical tent as the rain came down harder.

Elara and Sam each took a woman's arm, guiding them through the camp, but Sam's hesitation was evident. His eyes flickered toward the new arrivals with something unreadable, his jaw tight. Clarisse knew what he was thinking.

Can we even afford to take them in?

The weight of that question sat heavy on her shoulders too. Supplies were already stretched thin. Taking in twenty-two plus more people—wounded, starving, traumatized—was an enormous risk. But they weren't in the business of turning away people in need. At least, Clarisse wasn't.

She shot Sam a warning glance, then turned her full attention back to the situation at hand.

Inside the tent, Macy was already in motion, clearing a space on the worn medical cots as McCann laid the infant down. The baby was far too still. Too quiet.

Clarisse's heart pounded.

"She's barely breathing," McCann murmured, his voice hoarse. His hands hovered near the baby's chest, as if afraid to move her the wrong way. "I don't know if—"

"We're not losing her," Clarisse said sharply. "Not today."

She pressed two fingers against the tiny ribs, feeling for breath, for heartbeat. It was faint. Too faint.

"Come on, sweetheart," she whispered, already moving into action. "Stay with me."

Macy shoved a ragged towel into her hands. It wasn't ideal, but it was warm and dry. Clarisse wrapped the infant in it, trying to coax warmth into her fragile body.

Then the silence in the tent broke as one of the survivors, a woman with hollow cheeks and a desperate look in her eyes, stepped forward. "Please," she gasped, her voice shaking. "Where is she?"

Clarisse glanced up. "Where's who?"

The woman's eyes darted wildly. "My sister. She was with the others. She was supposed to be with them on the boat."

A heavy silence filled the tent.

Clarisse felt the shift in the air. *They don't know.*

The survivors—exhausted, battered, free for the first time in months, years maybe—were only just realizing that they were free.

But Graham's group was still out there.

And there were no guarantees.

Clarisse swallowed hard, keeping her focus on the baby, forcing herself to work. There was a rising tension in the room, one she couldn't deal with right now. But it needed to be addressed. Soon.

McCann stepped forward, putting a firm hand on the woman's shoulder. "They're coming," he said, his voice calm, steady. "They're coming back."

The woman nodded, but tears filled her eyes. Clarisse had

seen that kind of hope before—the kind that barely held itself together with fraying edges.

Hope was fragile. But it was all they had.

Behind them, Sam exhaled sharply. "How many more mouths are we supposed to feed?"

Clarisse's head snapped up. "Are you seriously asking that right now?"

Sam crossed his arms. "I'm asking how we're supposed to survive if we keep taking in more people when we can barely feed the ones we already have."

"You're free to leave," she snapped.

Sam stiffened. The tension between them was razor-thin.

Macy suddenly pushed through, brushing past Sam and heading straight for the radio. "I need to get some names out," she muttered. "Some of these ladies may have relatives nearby."

When Macy entered the comms room, Paige, who had been silent until now, lifted her head from where she sat by the radio, Scout curled at her feet. "No."

Macy paused. "Excuse me?"

Paige didn't blink. "No. Don't touch it. I'm waiting for Graham."

Macy scoffed. "It doesn't work like that, Paige. The radio isn't a one-way line."

"I don't care," Paige said, her voice steel. "We. Wait."

Macy groaned, rubbing her temples. "Are you serious right now?"

Paige didn't move.

Clarisse heard yelling from the comms room. She wanted to intervene, but she was too busy pressing against the baby's mouth, breathing for her, willing her tiny lungs to work. The argument at the radio continued in the background, Macy getting increasingly frustrated, Paige getting increasingly stubborn.

Then, suddenly—

A *gasp*.

Clarisse's heart stuttered. The baby twitched, then let out a tiny, fragile cry.

"She's breathing," Clarisse whispered.

McCann let out a shaky breath. Elara exhaled in relief. Even Sam looked away, pressing his lips together.

The storm outside raged on.

Then the radio *crackled*.

The entire tent went silent.

A garbled voice cut through the static.

At first, it was too broken to make out, but then— "to shore— Bowman Bay. We need."

Clarisse's blood ran cold.

It was Graham.

Macy slowly turned toward Paige, a small, triumphant smirk forming.

Paige didn't take her eyes off the radio.

Clarisse swallowed hard.

Now they had a choice to make.

Now everything changed.

CHAPTER 21 - STRANDED AT BOWMAN BAY

The boat was already half-submerged when they hit the shallows. Graham barely had time to grab Lawoaka and her baby before the cold salt water swallowed them both whole. The current slammed against his body, dragging him down, but he fought his way to the surface, gasping for air as waves crashed over his head.

"Get to shore!" he bellowed, his voice barely audible over the wind and churning sea.

He couldn't see all of them—not in the dim light, not in the chaos—but he could hear their frantic splashing, the coughing and choking as they fought against the water. The shoreline was just ahead, a jagged strip of rocks and sand.

Graham tightened his grip on Lawoaka. "Don't panic," he turned her around to float on her back, the infant to her chest, and kicked hard. His muscles burned, but after what felt like an eternity, his feet scraped against the seabed. He staggered onto the beach, hauling her and the child with him, coughing up seawater as he collapsed onto his knees.

Arlen had pulled two ashore. He and Graham went out again, and then one by one, the others made it, gasping and shivering as they dragged themselves further onto the shore.

"Lawoaka?" Graham turned his head, searching the dark shapes sprawled across the sand.

She was there, soaked and shivering, but alive. The others too—most of them.

One body still floated in the surf.

Graham forced himself to his feet and stumbled forward, bracing against the wind. It was one of the women—Janey, he thought her name was. He pulled her out of the tide, checked for a pulse, but there was nothing. Her skin was too cold, her lips already turning blue.

He clenched his jaw. She had been alive when they left, when she was freed, but only for a few moments.

Now, she wasn't.

Arlen groaned beside him, dragging himself upright. "Where... the hell are we?"

Graham turned toward the trees. The cliffs of Deception Pass were too far east. They hadn't made it. They had been pushed south, caught in the currents. But he recognized the general landscape—the uneven tree line, the distant cliffs, the faint silhouette of a dock further down the coast.

Bowman Bay.

It was close enough to Deception Pass that they could try signaling, but there was no guarantee anyone would be looking for them. At least, not the friendly people.

Lawoaka pointed toward the tree line, where a faded wooden sign jutted from the ground. Ranger Station – 0.3 miles.

Graham wiped the water from his face. "We need shelter. Now."

The Ranger Station

The old station was barely standing. Half the windows were broken, the front door hung open, and the musty scent of decay filled the air.

But it had walls.

They piled inside, shivering uncontrollably. Lawoaka and two of the other women huddled near an old desk, while Arlen slumped against the wall, his breath ragged.

"We need fire," Graham muttered.

Arlen coughed. "We need dry wood first."

Graham's hands were numb, but he forced himself to move. There was a rusted metal filing cabinet in the corner, its drawers already half-open. Old papers. Maps. Anything that would burn.

Graham ripped one of the maps in half and started gathering more paper, his hands shaking but methodical.

Arlen found a rusty fire extinguisher, shook it, and tossed it aside. "No good. What else?"

Graham moved to the back of the station, scanning the shadows. Then, against the far wall, he saw it—a radio.

It was ancient, covered in dust, but it was still wired to a backup battery. He rushed toward it, flipping switches, twisting knobs.

Nothing.

He cursed under his breath, trying again. Static crackled faintly through the speakers, then cut out.

Lawoaka moved beside him and pointed at a sign. Emergency Power – Manual Activation Required.

"There's a generator," Graham realized.

Arlen pushed himself up. "Where?"

"Outside."

He grabbed a lantern from the supply shelf—miraculously, it still had oil—and stepped back into the rain.

The Generator

The shed behind the station was half-collapsed, vines growing through its frame. But the generator was there, rusted but intact.

Graham knelt, brushing debris away. It was gas-powered. He cursed. They had no fuel.

Arlen groaned. "You're kidding me."

Graham ran a hand over the old metal casing, thinking. Sometimes, emergency fuel caches were stored nearby. If the ranger station had been maintained before the collapse, there was a chance…

"Help me check," he said.

They searched the shed, then the back of the station. Nothing.

Then Lawoaka pointed toward a locked storage box near the ranger's desk.

Arlen didn't hesitate—he grabbed the fire extinguisher and slammed it against the lock. Once. Twice. The metal bent, and the latch snapped free.

Graham pried the lid open.

Inside, beneath a pile of old blankets, was a single red gas can.

"Please don't be empty," Arlen muttered.

Graham unscrewed the cap and sniffed. The fuel inside was old but usable.

Arlen grinned. "Hell yeah."

They hauled it back outside, poured every last drop into the generator, and Graham grabbed the pull-start.

He braced himself, yanked hard—nothing.

Again.

Still nothing.

Arlen swore. "Come on, you bastard."

One more pull—the engine coughed, sputtered, then roared to life.

Inside, the radio crackled.

The Transmission

Graham ran inside, twisting the knobs until the static cleared. The signal was weak, but it was there.

"This is Graham..." He paused, forcing his voice steady. "Does anyone copy?"

Nothing.

He tried again.

Then—a faint voice.

"...Say again... barely hear you..."

His chest tightened. "Macy? Can you hear me?"

Static.

"...Graham?"

The voice was faint, cutting in and out, but it was her.

"We made it to shore," he said quickly. "Bowman Bay. We need—"

The radio cut out.

Graham twisted the knob. "Macy, do you copy?"

Silence.

Arlen tapped the radio, then shook his head. The power was dying.

Graham exhaled sharply. They had one transmission. That was it.

But it was enough.

He looked at Arlen. "Now we wait."

Outside, the rain fell harder, drumming against the roof like a heartbeat.

Somewhere, far beyond the waves, help was coming.

CHAPTER 22- A FRUSTRATING WAIT

The night had settled into an eerie stillness. The rain had tapered to a light drizzle, but the cold had sunk deep into Corey's bones. He and Tehya had huddled inside the gutted remains of the bullet-riddled truck, their makeshift shelter against the wind howling through Deception Pass.

Tehya had barely spoken in the last hour. She was curled up in the passenger seat, arms wrapped around herself, staring at nothing. Corey didn't know what to say, so he didn't push.

They were both just waiting.

Corey shifted slightly, adjusting his rifle across his lap. He wasn't quite asleep when the radio crackled in his hand. His eyes snapped open.

A burst of static, then—

"Corey? Are you there?"

Macy.

Tehya bolted upright beside him, suddenly alert. Corey fumbled for the radio, thumb pressing down the button. "Yeah, I'm here. Go ahead."

"We just heard from Graham."

Corey shot up so fast he smacked his head against the truck's crumpled roof. He ignored the pain. "What? Say that again?"

Macy's voice came clearer now, laced with relief. "Graham's alive. They made it to Bowman Bay."

Tehya gasped beside him, her fingers digging into Corey's sleeve.

Corey exhaled, the tension in his chest loosening—just slightly.

"Bowman Bay?" he repeated, already running calculations in his head. It wasn't that far. If he had enough fuel—

"Can you get to them?" Macy asked, urgency in her voice.

Corey hesitated. Could he?

He looked down at the radio, then back at Tehya. She was practically vibrating with hope, her eyes wide, pleading. She didn't have to say anything.

She needed him to say yes.

Corey sighed. "Hold on."

Ignoring the cold, he shoved open the rusted door and stepped out into the storm. The wind bit through his jacket as he crossed the gravel toward the boats. The rain had turned everything slick, and the dock swayed beneath his feet as he climbed aboard the first boat—their original. He popped the cap off the fuel tank and peered inside, shaking his head. Not enough.

Teeth gritted, he jumped to the second boat—the one they'd stolen. If they were lucky, maybe—

He unscrewed the cap, checked the fuel.

Not even close.

Corey let out a slow breath, cursing under it.

He turned back toward the truck, where Tehya stood watching him from the open door. She must have seen the answer in his expression, because her face fell as he lifted his hand and gave her a thumbs-down.

Defeat slumped her shoulders.

Corey climbed back into the truck, shaking rain from his hair, and grabbed the radio.

"No go," he told Macy. "I checked both tanks—there's no way we'd make the round trip. I'm glad they're okay, but we'll have to wait until someone brings fuel."

Macy exhaled, disappointed. "Damn."

Corey sighed, running a hand through his damp hair. "Tell Graham to sit tight. The storm's still bad anyway. Better to wait for calmer seas."

A pause, then—

"Agreed," Macy said.

Then another voice crackled onto the radio.

"Corey."

Sam.

Corey straightened. "Go ahead."

Sam's voice was steady, but Corey could hear the movement in the background—people gearing up, getting ready. "I'll bring fuel. And a truck to get everyone back."

Corey's chest eased a little at that. At least something was in motion.

"How soon?" he asked.

"Few hours," Sam answered. "Maybe more, depending on the road. Sit tight."

Corey glanced at Tehya. She had turned back toward the water, her arms crossed, shoulders stiff. She hated waiting.

So did he.

But they had no choice.

"Roger that," Corey muttered into the radio. "We'll be here."

The radio went silent.

Corey leaned back against the seat, exhausted but unable to close his eyes. He wasn't sure which was worse—the storm outside or the one brewing inside Tehya.

The minutes stretched on, and the air inside the truck grew thick with unspoken thoughts. The rain tapped lightly against the metal roof, a metronome of their waiting. Every so often, Tehya shifted, her fingers tapping restlessly against her knee.

"I hate this," she muttered finally, breaking the silence.

Corey turned to her, noting the tension in her jaw. "I know."

She let out a frustrated breath, running a hand through her damp hair. "Sitting here, doing nothing, while they're out there…"

"They're alive," Corey reminded her. "That's something."

She nodded but didn't look convinced. "Doesn't mean they're safe."

Corey didn't argue. He knew better. Instead, he leaned forward, adjusting the rifle across his lap, his fingers gripping the cold metal just a little tighter.

"We'll get them," he said, more to himself than to her.

Tehya turned to look at him then, something unreadable in her eyes. For the first time that night, she didn't look so lost in her own thoughts.

Another moment of silence passed between them before she exhaled and pulled her coat tighter around herself. "Yeah," she said softly. "We will."

And so, they waited.

CHAPTER 23- THE FLICKERING LIGHT

The ranger station was a husk of what it once was—its walls lined with long-forgotten maps and notices, all curling at the edges from years of neglect. Graham pulled the threadbare wool blanket tighter around Lawoaka and her child, willing his own body heat to seep into her shivering frame. The baby nestled between them whimpered softly, its tiny fingers gripping at the fabric of Graham's coat. Lawoaka didn't speak. She barely moved, except for the faint rise and fall of her chest.

The cold had crept in like a living thing, coiling around their bones, seeping through layers of scavenged clothing. Every breath was a visible cloud in the dim light, the air crisp with the scent of dust, old wood, and something metallic that Graham suspected was lingering blood from past conflicts.

Arlen moved through the cramped space, handing out blankets that were little more than dusty rags. He draped one over a young woman huddled in the corner, then another, who sat with her knees drawn up to her chest. She gave him a quiet nod of thanks, but her eyes were fixed on the boarded-up window, as if she expected something—or someone—to come through it at any moment.

"Not much," Arlen muttered, holding up the last blanket before tossing it over Graham's shoulders. "But it's something."

Graham shifted slightly, adjusting his grip on Lawoaka. Her trembling had lessened some, but her skin was still too cold. The baby was bundled tight in whatever scraps of fabric they'd managed to find, but Graham wasn't sure it would be enough.

"We need heat," he said. His voice was quiet, but it cut through the room like an order.

Arlen met his gaze, then looked around the room. "Not much to burn."

Graham's eyes landed on a rusted metal barrel in the corner. He gently eased Lawoaka to the side, making sure she stayed wrapped up before he got to his feet. The barrel was dented, one side nearly caved in, but it would work.

"We use what we can," Graham said.

One woman rose, already peeling away from the group. "I'll find something," she said, voice hushed but determined. Before he could protest, she slipped through the station's back door into the darkness beyond.

Graham wanted to stop her, but there were other concerns at hand. He grabbed a rusted-out chair, its legs barely holding together, and began breaking it apart. The wood was brittle but dry—perfect for kindling. Arlen took the hint and did the same, moving to the far side of the room where an old shelf leaned against the wall.

Within minutes, they had a small pile of burnable material. Graham knelt beside the barrel, pulling a lighter from his coat pocket. He'd been rationing it, using it only when necessary. The fluid was nearly gone, but he didn't hesitate.

A flick, a spark, and then—fire.

The flames caught quickly, licking at the dry wood, filling the room with the scent of scorched dust and something bitter that Graham didn't want to identify. The warmth was weak at first, barely touching the icy air, but it was enough.

Lawoaka stirred, her eyes fluttering open. Her gaze landed on the fire, then on Graham. She didn't speak, but she pulled her baby closer, tucking her chin over the child's head.

Graham sat back, rubbing his hands together and extending them toward the flames. Around him, the others did the same, inching forward, the fire a beacon in the cold.

The woman returned a few minutes later, her arms full of scavenged wood—half-rotten boards, broken chair legs, even a few old ranger manuals.

"Best I could find," she murmured, dropping the pile beside the barrel.

Graham gave her a nod of approval, feeding a few more pieces into the fire. The flames flared brighter, warmth stretching into the corners of the room.

For the first time in hours, the tension in the room eased—just a little.

Outside, the wind howled, a sharp, cutting sound against

the walls of the station. Snowflakes drifted in through the cracks in the boarded-up windows, dusting the floor in a fine layer of white.

Graham let out a slow breath. The fire wouldn't last forever, and neither would the safety of this place. But for now, they had warmth. They had each other.

It would have to be enough.

The crackling fire was the only sound for a while, its warmth slow but steady, stretching fingers of heat into the coldest parts of the room. Arlen shifted next to him, reaching for his pack and pulling out a battered tin cup. He poured a small ration of water from his canteen, offering it to Lawoaka.

She hesitated at first, blinking as though it had taken her a moment to register what was happening. Then, weakly, she accepted it, taking small sips as she cradled her child tighter against her chest.

"Drink slow," Arlen warned. "Last thing we need is you getting sick on top of everything else."

Graham watched as Lawoaka's grip on the cup steadied. Her hands weren't trembling as much. That was something.

"We'll stay through the night," Arlen murmured, glancing at the others huddled around the fire. "Come first light, we move."

Graham nodded. It was the only option. Staying too long in one place was dangerous. The fire was a necessity, but it was also a beacon for anyone close enough to see the glow.

He flexed his fingers, the heat slowly bringing sensation back into them. Despite the circumstances, despite the danger still lingering just outside these fragile walls, there was a small moment of peace in the quiet crackling of the fire.

Lawoaka's baby let out a small, sleepy sigh against her chest. Graham let himself relax—just for a moment.

Morning would come soon enough. And with it, the next fight.

For now, the fire burned, and they were still here.

CHAPTER 24 - THE WEIGHT OF DECISIONS

Sam adjusted the strap of the gas canister over his shoulder and took a deep breath of the cold morning air. The camp was already stirring behind him—a collection of low voices, the shuffle of boots on frost-covered ground, and the sharp metallic clang of someone checking their weapon. The storm had passed, leaving behind a clear but biting sky, the kind that carried the promise of another brutal winter.

Beside him, Bang sat on an overturned crate, his rifle balanced across his lap, eyes scanning the perimeter like a damn machine. His posture was rigid, but exhaustion hung off of him like a worn-out coat. Sam had been around long enough to recognize when a man was running on fumes.

Bang hadn't left his post in over twenty-four hours.

Sam exhaled, glancing over toward Addy, who stood just a few feet away, arms crossed, her expression an even mix of frustration and concern. Her dark hair was pulled back into a tight braid, but strands had worked their way loose, clinging to her face in the stiff wind. She looked so much like her mother it sent a pang through Sam's chest.

"Bang, you need to sleep," Addy said, her voice firm but not unkind. "You can't keep watch forever. Let me take a shift."

Bang didn't even glance her way. "Not happening."

Addy huffed, stepping closer. "You're barely standing. You think I can't handle this? You trained me, remember?"

Sam watched as Bang finally shifted, his gaze flickering toward her, jaw tightening. "It's not about whether you can handle it. It's about whether you should."

That was the wrong thing to say.

Addy squared her shoulders, stepping right into Bang's space. "You're gonna collapse at this rate. If you won't go sleep in a cot, at least go sleep next to the baby. He needs you awake later, not dead on your feet now."

Bang's grip tightened on his rifle. "I'll sleep when the shift is covered."

"You're impossible," Addy snapped, throwing her hands in the air.

Sam chuckled, shaking his head. "You know," he mused, setting his gas canister down on the tailgate of the truck, "her mother once slipped something into my coffee to get me to sleep. Don't put it past her to do the same to you."

Bang finally looked at Sam, eyes narrowing. "She wouldn't."

Sam just smiled. "You wanna take that risk?"

Bang let out a slow breath, his hands flexing on his rifle. "Fine. One hour. That's it."

Addy smirked. "Sure. Whatever you say."

Bang grumbled under his breath, finally pushing to his feet. He handed his rifle off to another guard and stalked toward the shelter where the baby was sleeping. Addy watched him go, a satisfied smirk on her face before turning back to Sam.

"Thanks," she muttered.

Sam chuckled again, shaking his head. "You're just like your mother."

She rolled her eyes but didn't argue.

With Bang finally resting, Sam turned back to the task at hand—loading up the truck with enough fuel to get Corey to Graham and back. The boat fuel sloshed inside the heavy-duty canisters as he strapped them down in the bed of the truck, making sure everything was secure.

Corey approached as Sam tightened the last strap. The drive had been peaceful, almost eerily so. The early morning fog had hung low over the road, the frost shimmering on the trees like nature was oblivious to the chaos that surrounded them. It reminded Sam of the quiet mornings before the world went to hell, when a drive like that would have been just another day of work, not a moment of reprieve before heading back into the storm.

Now, standing at the entrance to Deception Pass, the contrast was jarring. The tension was palpable, a heavy weight in the air. Tehya was a few steps behind Corey, arms crossed, her jaw set in defiance.

"Tehya, you have to go back with Sam," Corey said firmly. "My mission to get Graham and the others might take a while. Maybe even overnight."

Tehya's expression hardened. "Then I'll go with you."

Corey shook his head. "We can't be so strung out and thin—that makes us a target. And Sam's truck will be a target if it just sits here. If Graham were here, he'd never let you stay. You know that."

She hesitated, her fingers curling into fists. "I don't like it."

"Neither do I," Corey admitted. "But I'll radio in when I find them. You need to be back at camp, keeping things steady. We can't afford to lose anyone else."

Tehya exhaled through her nose, clearly fighting her instincts. Finally, she gave a curt nod. "Fine. But you better call in the second you make contact."

"I will," Corey promised.

Sam gave Tehya a reassuring nod as she reluctantly climbed into the truck. As she settled in, Sam handed Corey the last gas canister. Corey took it without a word and moved toward the boat, unscrewing the cap of one of the tanks. The faint smell of fuel filled the air as he carefully poured the contents inside. Once finished, he screwed the cap back on and handed the empty canister back to Sam, who placed it in the truck bed.

Sam stood there for a moment, watching as Corey crouched down and worked on getting the boat's engine running again. The soft sputtering sound turned into a steady hum, and Sam knew Corey would be gone soon.

Corey glanced up and gave a small wave toward Tehya in

the truck. She didn't wave back. Sam smirked, shaking his head. Addy had been a teenager once, too, but Tehya—Tehya was a handful. "You're making the right call."

She didn't respond, just stared out the window as Corey stepped back, giving Sam a silent nod of thanks.

Sam exhaled through his nose, then climbed into the seat, noting that Corey looked even more sleep-deprived than Bang. And Tehya didn't look much better. He lingered for a moment, watching as Corey's boat disappeared into the misty horizon, the hum of the engine fading into the distance.

With a final glance, Sam shifted the truck into gear and pulled away, Tehya beside him, sullen as ever. The silence stretched between them, heavy with unspoken frustration on both ends.

CHAPTER 25 - NO WAY OUT

The storm had settled into a steady drizzle, but the cold was relentless, clinging to everything like an unshakable omen. Graham adjusted his hold on Lawoaka and her baby, shifting his body to shield them from the damp air seeping through the cracks of the old ranger station. He could feel the woman shivering against him, her body exhausted, the baby barely stirring.

Across the dim room, the others sat in silence, wrapped in the musty, dust-caked blankets Arlen had scrounged from an old supply closet. Their faces were hollowed by exhaustion, cheeks gaunt from months of starvation and fear.

Graham's eyes drifted across the room—Lawoaka wasn't the only one shivering. The women sat huddled together, their expressions blank, hollow. Not from the cold, but from the weight of what they had endured. What they had survived.

A soft, tired cry broke through the stillness.

The baby stirred weakly, her tiny fingers clutching at the fabric of Lawoaka's shirt. Graham instinctively rocked her, his hands rough but gentle. The sound barely registered to the others. They were too far gone—too frozen, too drained, too lost in the haze of exhaustion.

Only Arlen moved, his eyes flicking toward the door, shoulders stiff.

Graham let out a slow breath, staring into the rusted barrel where the fire flickered, its glow barely warming the room. The flames sent erratic shadows dancing along the walls, but even with the fire, something felt wrong.

The air was thick with something other than cold. A warning. A shift.

Graham scanned the room, and that's when he realized—no one was sleeping.

Even the most exhausted survivors sat awake, their eyes darting toward the boarded-up windows, toward the weakly creaking door.

Then he heard it.

A low, distant hum.

At first, he thought it was the wind—just the soft howl of the night slipping through the trees. But the sound wasn't shifting. It wasn't carrying like the rain against the roof.

It was steady. Consistent. Getting closer.

Graham stiffened.

His gut twisted.

That was no wind.

It was a motor.

A boat.

He went completely still.

Across the room, Arlen's head jerked up. His eyes met Graham's, and they both knew.

This wasn't Corey.

Corey didn't have the fuel for a return trip so soon. Even if they'd left the moment they'd heard Graham's radio call, there was no way they could have made it this fast.

Which meant...

This wasn't their people.

Graham carefully eased Lawoaka and the baby next to one of the women. The mother barely registered the movement. She clung to the child, rocking her absently, staring at the floor like she was trapped in another world.

Graham grabbed his rifle and motioned for Arlen to follow. Quietly, they moved toward the shattered front windows, keeping low.

The rain had softened into a fine mist, making the water beyond the shore glisten under the moonlight. The waves rolled in, lapping quietly at the rocky beach.

Then he saw it.

Not just one boat.

Several.

Graham's stomach twisted into a knot so tight he felt like he couldn't breathe.

He counted four.

Sleek. Dark. Armed.

They were gliding toward the shore, their hulls barely cutting through the waves.

Arlen muttered a curse under his breath, and Graham's grip on his rifle tightened.

Then, the first robed figure stepped onto the beach.

Graham didn't recognize him.

Neither did Arlen.

More draped figures followed. Men. Armed. Glaring at the remains of their boat washed into the rocky shore.

Not scavengers.

Not opportunists.

These terrorists were hunting them.

Graham's mind whirled. They'd found them.

Then he heard them speak.

A quiet, clipped murmur.

Arabic.

Graham's heart pounded against his ribs.

They were here.

Arlen's breathing slowed, steady but deliberate, like a man who knew he was facing death but was preparing to meet it head-on. Graham felt the same.

They had no way of getting everyone out of the station.

Not the women.

Not the babies.

They were too weak.

There was no way to warn anyone.

No time to run.

They were trapped.

Cornered.

A part of Graham had always known it would end like this. He wasn't a fool—he knew there were too many moving pieces, too many variables. He'd pushed his luck one too many times.

His mind raced through options.

Theya and Bang. Paige and the baby he'd never know.

None of them were good.

He turned to Arlen. Kept his voice low.

"Get them out."

Arlen barely moved.

"Graham—"

"There's no time to argue."

Graham grabbed Arlen's rifle, slinging it over his own shoulder.

"I'll buy you as much time as I can."

Arlen's jaw clenched.

He understood.

Graham didn't wait for him to argue.

Didn't wait for reason to step in.

Instead, he took a step forward.

Into the night.

Toward the boats.

Toward the men.

His fingers tightened around the triggers.

There was no way out.

But at least…

He could give the others one.

CHAPTER 26 - THE LAST STAND

Graham moved like a ghost through the ruined forest, his boots silent against the earth. He could hear the hushed breathing of the women and the occasional rustle of cloth as someone shifted through the trees behind him. Despite their exhaustion, no one spoke. Fear had bound them tighter than any rope ever could.

The rain had picked up again, a steady, insistent drizzle that made the earth damp and the air thick with the scent of pine and salt. It should have been soothing. Instead, it felt suffocating.

Arlen crouched beside him, took up Graham's binoculars, his face grim as he peeked between the tree balms. "They're still unloading. Looks like… a dozen, maybe more."

Graham clenched his jaw. "Armed?"

Arlen nodded. "Heavily. And moving like they know what they're doing."

Graham exhaled slowly. No hesitation. No wasted movement. These men weren't here by accident. They were looking for them.

He looked back at the others as their shadows dimmed in the trees. "How many are still strong enough to move a mile or two?"

Arlen's face darkened. "Four, maybe five. The rest are too weak, too cold. And the babies—"

They both turned to where Lawoaka cradled her child, rocking gently as she waited for Arlen. The baby had finally quieted, but her tiny body was still wracked with shivers. If they had to run, she wouldn't make it far.

Graham's chest tightened. They weren't going to outrun this.

Another voice—low, commanding—carried through the mist. Arabic. Graham didn't understand the words, but the tone was clear. Orders.

He turned to Arlen. "Time's up. Get them out."

Arlen stiffened. "Graham, we can fight. We have—"

"No. We can't. And we won't get another chance." Graham tightened his grip on his rifle, his decision already made. "Get them to safety."

Arlen hesitated, his hands flexing into fists. The idea of retreating—leaving someone behind—was anathema. But Arlen had been fighting long enough to know when a battle was lost before it began.

Graham gave him a firm nod. "You can still save them. I'll buy you time."

Arlen's jaw clenched, but finally, he gave a curt nod. He

moved quickly, whispering to the stronger women, guiding them further where the forest thickened into shadow.

Graham turned back toward the shore. The first figures had begun to fan out, boots sinking into the damp sand. He caught a glimpse of dark tactical gear, weapons glinting under the moonlight.

They were close now.

Graham took a deep breath, adjusting the weight of the rifle against his shoulder. He'd been in worse situations before.

This time, he was all that stood between a group of defenseless women and children, and certain death.

He took one last look at the ranger station, ensuring Arlen and the others had disappeared into the night.

Then he stepped into the open.

The men reacted instantly.

A shout. Weapons raised. A flashlight cut through the rain, landing squarely on Graham's chest.

"Don't move!"

Graham stopped but didn't lower his rifle. He kept his hands steady, feet planted firmly in the mud. The leader stepped forward, a man with sharp features and calculating eyes. He spoke again in Arabic, then switched to English.

"Who are you?"

Graham didn't answer.

The man studied him, head tilting slightly. "Where are the others?"

Graham let out a breath, slow and deliberate. He needed to buy more time. "No one else. Just me."

The leader's lips curled in amusement. "Lies." He gestured behind him. Two men peeled off, moving toward the station.

Graham's muscles tensed. He couldn't let them go inside. Couldn't let them follow the others.

His grip tightened on the trigger.

And then he fired.

The crack of the rifle split the night. One of the men dropped before he could react, the other staggering back with a sharp cry.

Then hell erupted.

Gunfire tore through the silence, the flashes lighting up the rain-soaked night like bursts of lightning. Graham dove behind a rotting log, feeling the impact of bullets splintering the wood above his head.

He took a deep breath, exhaled, and returned fire.

One. Two. Another dropped.

But there were too many.

Graham gritted his teeth, knowing this wasn't a fight he could win. He just had to hold out long enough.

A burst of gunfire struck near his foot, and he rolled, landing hard in the mud. He could hear them moving in, their boots crunching against the wet ground. He only had a few bullets left.

His chest heaved as he prepared for one final stand.

And then—

A sound. Distant but growing louder. Engines.

Graham's eyes flicked toward the shoreline.

Another boat.

For a moment, he thought it was more of them—another wave of enemies. But then he saw it.

A spotlight.

A Kiwi voice over a megaphone, cutting through the gunfire.

"Drop your weapons! Hands in the air!"

Graham nearly collapsed with relief.

It was Corey.

It was his people.

The enemy faltered, hesitation flickering in their movements. They hadn't expected reinforcements.

Graham took the chance. He fired off another shot, hitting one in the leg.

The others turned, assessing their new threat. One of them barked an order in Arabic, and then, just like that, they were retreating.

The boats pushed off the shore, engines roaring to life as they sped into the darkness.

Graham slumped against the log, breathless. His fingers were numb around the rifle. His body ached from exhaustion, but he couldn't afford to stop.

Corey's boat hit the shore hard, the spotlight like a sun blaze upon the rocky shore.

"Graham!" Corey's voice was sharp with concern.

Graham exhaled, forcing himself to his feet. He swayed slightly but caught himself. "You took your damn time."

Corey let out a breath of relief. "Yeah, well. You're lucky I did."

Graham glanced at the tree line. Arlen and the others had made it.

He let out a slow, measured breath. "We need to move."

Corey nodded. "Let's get them the hell out of here."

CHAPTER 27 - THE COST OF SURVIVAL

The echoes of the last gunshot still hung in the damp air as Corey adjusted his grip on his rifle, scanning the inky shore for any lingering threats. The enemy had retreated, vanishing into the darkness the same way they had arrived—silent and fast. It wasn't over, not by a long shot, but for now, they had bought themselves a few precious moments to regroup.

Graham pressed a hand against his ribs, wincing as he pushed himself to his feet. The adrenaline had masked the worst of it, but now that the fight was over, pain settled in like an old enemy. He turned toward Corey, nodding in silent appreciation.

"You're late," Graham rasped.

Corey snorted. "Traffic was hell."

The tension eased slightly, but only for a moment. The real problem wasn't the fight—it was what came next. Graham turned his attention toward the tree line where Arlen had disappeared. He needed to get to them before it was too late.

"Where's Arlen?" Corey asked, following his gaze.

Graham wiped the rain from his face, feeling the weight of exhaustion settle in. "Deeper in the woods. He took the women. Where's Teyha?"

Corey exhaled. "With Sam. We better find them before those bastards come back."

He wasn't wrong. They had driven them off, but not killed them all. They would regroup and return. And when they did, they wouldn't make the same mistakes.

"We need to move," Graham said. "Now."

Corey took point, rifle raised as they made their way into the forest. The storm had passed, but the ground was still slick with mud, each step uncertain. Graham forced himself forward, ignoring the dull ache in his ribs.

They moved quickly, following the faint path Arlen had carved through the underbrush. It wasn't long before they spotted movement ahead—Arlen and the women, huddled together beneath the skeletal remains of an overturned logging truck. Relief flashed through Graham, but it was short-lived.

One of the women was on the ground, unmoving.

Graham was at her side in seconds. "What happened?"

Arlen shook his head. "She collapsed halfway here. I tried to carry her, but—" His voice trailed off, his expression grim. "She was too far gone."

Graham checked for a pulse, but he already knew. She was cold. Her lips tinged blue from more than just the cold.

"We keep moving," Corey said. "We don't have time."

The remaining women clung to each other, eyes wide with exhaustion and fear. Graham scanned them quickly. They were all weak, malnourished, but still moving. They could make it—if they hurried.

"We're getting out of here," he told them, his voice firm. "Stay close and don't stop for anything."

Corey nodded. "We'll have to get to the water."

Arlen sighed. "Of course we do."

They didn't waste another second.

The march back toward the shore was slow, the terrain working against them with every step. Graham kept his rifle ready, every rustling branch sending his heart into overdrive. The enemy had retreated, but they weren't gone. They were waiting.

By the time they reached the edge of the trees, the sky had begun to lighten. Dawn. Graham hadn't even realized how much time had passed.

Corey crouched beside him, scanning the shoreline. "Still clear."

"For now," Graham muttered.

The wind off the water was sharp, carrying the scent of salt and damp earth. Graham turned toward the group. "We wait here until our path to the boat is safe."

The women sank into the underbrush without argument, exhaustion keeping them silent.

Arlen nudged Graham. "You hear that?"

Graham frowned, listening. And then—he did.

A boat.

The low hum of an engine carried over the water, steady and deliberate. It was moving toward them, not away. Graham tensed, motioning for the others to stay low. Corey adjusted his grip on his rifle, eyes narrowing as the shape of the boat became clearer against the faint morning light.

Graham pressed himself lower against the wet earth, every muscle locked tight. If it wasn't their ride, they were in serious trouble.

Then, through the mist, a familiar voice crackled over a handheld radio.

"Graham, you there?"

Relief washed over him like a wave.

Corey exhaled. "That's Sam."

Graham reached for his radio, clicking it on. "We're here."

"Good," Sam's voice came back. "We're approaching fast. You got company?"

Graham's gaze flickered back toward the trees, scanning for movement. "Not yet. But they're not far."

"Copy that. Get everyone ready to move."

Graham turned to Arlen and Corey. "We get them off the boat fast. No hesitations."

Arlen nodded and moved toward the women, helping them to their feet, whispering encouragement. Corey kept his weapon up, watching the tree line, his body tense. Every second felt stretched too thin, the weight of what could go wrong pressing against them.

Then, a sound. Distant, but distinct.

A snap of a branch.

Graham's stomach tightened. He raised his rifle, scanning the tree line. Nothing yet, but they were close. Too close.

The boat's motor grew louder as it cut through the waves, pushing toward shore at full speed.

"Move!" Graham barked.

The women stumbled forward, pushing through exhaustion and fear. Arlen and Corey helped them down the embankment, the wind from the boat's approach whipping through their soaked clothes.

Graham took up the rear, his heart hammering as he backed toward the shoreline.

Then, just as the first woman stepped into the shallow surf—

A gunshot rang out.

Dirt kicked up inches from Graham's feet. He spun, firing blindly into the tree line. Shadows moved between the trunks, figures shifting in the mist.

"Get them on the boat!" he shouted.

Corey fired twice, dropping one of the attackers. Arlen was already in the water, hauling the women onto the deck. Sam was at the bow, covering them with his own rifle.

Another gunshot. Then another.

A cry of pain—one of the women.

"Dammit!" Graham growled, unloading another shot as he covered their retreat. The boat rocked violently as Sam pushed the engine harder, the spray of seawater stinging Graham's face as he grabbed the railing and hauled himself up.

Corey was the last one on, turning to fire one final shot

before dropping onto the deck beside Graham, breathing hard.

The boat pulled away, the shore fading into the mist. The enemy didn't follow. They just stood there, watching.

Watching them escape.

Graham collapsed onto the deck, his chest rising and falling in heavy breaths. His ribs ached, his muscles burned, but they had made it.

For now.

Corey sat beside him, gripping his rifle like a lifeline. "That was too damn close."

Graham nodded, staring at the shrinking shore. "Yeah."

He exhaled, shutting his eyes for just a moment.

Too damn close. Now if they could just get everyone out of the forest and to the boat and make it back to Deception Pass in one piece before the enemy returned.

CHAPTER 28 - THE RACE AGAINST TIME

The old truck rattled and groaned beneath Sam's hands as he gripped the wheel, pushing it as fast as he dared. The rain had turned the dirt roads to thick mud, and every dip and rise in the terrain sent a fresh spray of water and grime against the windshield. His breath came in steady beats, his focus locked on the road ahead. Tehya had slept most of the ride home, her arms crossed tight over her chest, her face half-buried in the thick fabric of her jacket. The silence between them had stretched long, but Sam had let it be. She'd agreed to return to camp, but he could tell she hated it.

As soon as he pulled into Graham's camp, Macy was already waiting.

"We just got word—they're on their way back," Macy said, urgency lacing her voice. "Sam, you have to turn around and go."

Tehya sat up straighter, her eyes narrowing. "Then I'm coming with him."

Macy didn't hesitate. Now was not the time. She yanked the passenger door open and pulled Tehya out before she could move. "No, you're not."

Tehya jerked her arm back, scowling. "I could've helped."

"You can help by staying here," Macy shot back. "We can't afford to stretch ourselves thin, and Sam needs to move. Right now."

Sam exhaled sharply, rubbing his hand down his face. "You serious?"

Macy nodded. "They need you, Sam. Corey's stuck. You have to go back now."

Tehya huffed but didn't argue further as Macy dragged her toward the command tent. Sam shifted the truck into gear and hauled ass the way he came. The early morning fog had hung low over the road, the frost shimmering on the trees like nature was oblivious to the chaos that surrounded them. It reminded Sam of the quiet mornings before the world went to hell, when a drive like that would have been just another day of work, not a moment of reprieve before heading back into the storm.

But this time, the enemy had moved in.

The hour-long drive back had been eerily quiet, the kind of silence that settled in just before disaster struck. The stretch of road had felt almost peaceful, the trees standing tall and undisturbed, the frost still glistening untouched by chaos. But as Sam neared Deception Pass, that peace shattered. The time it had taken him to turn around and return had given the enemy just enough time to move in, setting up positions and closing in on their target.

Now, standing at the entrance to Deception Pass, the contrast was jarring. The tension was palpable, a heavy weight in the air. Fires flickered in the distance, the shadows of figures moving between them. He knew better than to trust the silence.

Then, just as he was about to make a decision—

BOOM.

The explosion came from ahead, lighting up the night sky.

Sam's heart slammed against his ribs as he hit the brakes, the truck skidding sideways in the mud. The distant glow of fire illuminated the treetops, and he knew.

Graham's pick-up point had been compromised. They knew their destination was Deception Pass.

"Son of a—"

Sam grabbed the radio, flipping it to the open channel. "Macy! Get Corey on the damn radio! Something's happened!"

Static.

His heart pounded.

He didn't wait for a response. He shifted the truck into gear and made his choice.

He was going straight through.

The trees blurred past as he floored the gas, the truck roaring forward. If the enemy wanted to stop him, they'd have to try harder than that.

As he sped toward the firelight, his mind raced through the possibilities. If Graham and the others had been caught in that blast, he was already too late. If they were still alive, they wouldn't be for long.

A sharp burst of gunfire snapped through the night. Muzzle flashes from the tree line flickered like fireflies, popping in and out of the darkness.

Sam ducked lower in his seat and pressed the accelerator harder, gripping the wheel like a lifeline. Bullets pelted the truck, punching through the body with metallic clangs. The windshield cracked, a spiderweb fracture creeping across the glass.

"Not today, you bastards," Sam growled.

He reached for the rifle on the seat beside him, slinging it over his shoulder. He couldn't stop—not now—but he needed to even the odds. He braced the wheel with one knee, grabbed the rifle one-handed, and fired a shot through the shattered window toward the muzzle flashes.

The kick nearly sent the truck swerving into a ditch, but he corrected just in time.

More figures ahead—silhouettes against the burning wreckage of what looked like an abandoned outpost. They were moving fast, some scrambling for cover, others raising weapons.

Sam knew what that meant.

They weren't expecting a truck to come barreling straight at them.

"Hope you're ready for company," he muttered to no one in particular.

Then he slammed the accelerator to the floor.

The truck lurched forward, a beast unleashed. The first

enemy barely had time to react before the bumper clipped him, sending him sprawling into the mud. Another leapt to the side, firing wildly, bullets rattling against the truck bed.

Sam twisted the wheel hard, fishtailing into a group of stacked crates. The impact sent supplies flying, knocking over one of the makeshift barricades the enemy had set up.

CHAPTER 29 - THE ESCAPE FROM BOWMAN BAY

Graham could hear the voices of the enemy moving through the trees, fanning out along the shoreline. They were looking for them.

Graham turned to Arlen, who had a protective grip on one of the survivors. "We need to move. Now."

Corey was already ahead, eyes scanning the water where his boat was moored. "I don't like this," he muttered. "The tide's getting lower, and if they get to the boat before us, we're dead."

Graham knew he was right. They had two options—go fast and risk being spotted, or wait and risk being trapped.

"We don't have a choice," Graham said. "We move."

Arlen nodded, motioning for the women to stay close. Lawoaka clutched her baby to her chest, her eyes darting nervously toward the darkened tree line.

Corey led them down the narrow path toward the water,

his rifle raised, scanning ahead. Every step felt like a countdown. The air was thick with rain and the scent of saltwater, and the low rumble of waves breaking against the rocks was the only thing masking their hurried steps.

Then—voices.

Graham froze.

Ahead, just beyond the clearing, figures were moving toward their path. Five—maybe six men, all carrying rifles, their boots crunching against wet gravel.

They were between them and the boat.

Corey cursed under his breath. "We don't have time for this."

Graham glanced around, brain working fast. "Diversion," he said. "We need to draw them off."

Arlen looked at him. "And who's going to do that?"

Graham tightened his grip on his rifle. "I will."

"No way," Corey whispered harshly. "That's suicide."

"Not if you make it quick." Graham's gaze flicked to Arlen. "Get them on the boat. I'll meet you there."

Arlen hesitated.

Then, Lawoaka did something unexpected. She stepped forward and pressed a kiss to his cheek.

She didn't speak, but her eyes told him everything.

Come back.

Graham swallowed hard. He nodded.

Then, he took off into the darkness.

Graham moved quickly, staying low, weaving through the underbrush. He counted four men directly ahead, their backs turned as they scanned the shoreline. Two others were positioned closer to the shore, their rifles held loosely as they spoke in low tones.

He needed something loud.

He glanced down. His boot kicked against an old, rusted propane tank lying among the wreckage near a collapsed boathouse.

That'll do.

He adjusted his rifle, took careful aim, and pulled the trigger.

BOOM.

The explosion wasn't huge, but it was enough. The propane tank erupted with a burst of flame, sending the terrorists scrambling.

"Move!" Graham shouted.

From the tree line, Arlen and Corey rushed forward with the survivors, leading them down the path as the enemy scrambled to recover. Corey fired two quick shots, dropping one of the guards before they could react.

The second man spun, shouting a warning.

Graham hit him first.

He didn't wait to see if the others followed—he turned and sprinted after his group.

The boat engine roared to life just as he reached the dock. Corey was already at the controls, Arlen hauling people aboard.

Graham jumped, landing hard against the wooden edge as bullets chewed into the dock behind him.

Corey gunned the throttle.

The boat lurched forward, slicing through the dark water

as the shoreline erupted with gunfire. The last thing Graham saw before they rounded the cove was the enemy running after them, shouting in Arabic, raising their rifles.

They had escaped.

For now.

The only thing ahead of them was the short ride to Deception Pass.

CHAPTER 30 - THE ENEMY AT THE GATES

Every bump jarred Sam's already tense grip on the wheel. He had made it past the ambush—just barely. The road behind him was a twisted mess of bodies and overturned debris, but he'd pushed through. He was almost there.

Deception Pass was just ahead.

His radio crackled, Macy's voice cutting through the static.

"They made it out. Graham and the others are on their way."

Sam exhaled, tension easing slightly from his chest. That was the news he'd been waiting for.

He pressed the radio button. "Good. I'll be ready."

But even as he said it, a gnawing feeling settled in his gut. Something wasn't right. The mist ahead curled low over the road, clinging to the trees, swallowing the shapes in the distance. He had driven this path enough times to know what to expect, but something felt off.

Too quiet.

Too still.

He adjusted his grip on the wheel, easing his foot off the gas as he rounded the last bend before the entrance to Deception Pass.

Then, he saw them.

Figures.

At first, they were just dark shapes in the mist. His exhausted brain almost dismissed them as shadows, tricks of the dim light, but then one of them shifted, stepping into clearer view.

A man. Armed.

Then another.

Then more.

Sam's blood ran cold, and time slowed when he saw a figure slumped over on the side of the road, a pool of blood at the man's feet. A younger kid, long dark hair. Sam felt a tinge of guilt realizing the kid wasn't one of theirs. Had to be one of the Bellingham hippies, likely. He'd been tortured from the looks of things, but Sam couldn't think about that now.

Not his people.

His hand flew to the rifle in the passenger seat, but he knew he was outnumbered. He had counted at least a dozen figures so far, and more were emerging from the fog, moving in slow, deliberate steps.

His radio crackled again, Macy's voice coming through, frantic this time.

"Sam! They're taking fire! Graham's boat is under attack—"

The signal cut in and out, but Sam barely heard the rest.

Because now he could see them clearly—

And they weren't just waiting for him.

They were already here.

Deception Pass was compromised.

Sam clenched his teeth, his mind racing through options. He could slam the truck into them, but that would be suicide. They were too spread out. His rifle was within reach, but a straight gunfight wasn't going to cut it.

His fingers slid past the weapon, reaching instead for something more decisive.

A grenade.

"Sam! Are you there?" Macy's voice crackled in his ear.

Sam barely had time to press the radio. "I see them. Can't talk right now."

Then, just beyond the enemy line, Graham's boat tore into the harbor, two more trailing behind it—pursuers unloading bursts of gunfire into the water.

No time.

Sam ripped the pin, yanked open the truck door, and threw the grenade.

The dull *thunk* of it hitting the ground was followed by a half-second of stillness before—

BOOM!

A deafening explosion rocked the air, a flash of fire lighting up the fog-covered pass.

It stunned the armed men just long enough.

Sam didn't wait to see the outcome—he dove back into the truck, and hit the gas.

From the shoreline, Graham, Arlen, Corey, and the surviving prisoners witnessed the sudden fireball erupting near the entrance to Deception Pass.

Sam watched as Graham yelled something. They leaped from the boat, splashing through the shallows, and rushed toward the tree line for cover.

The enemy boats hesitated just for a moment, their crews startled by the explosion. But it wouldn't last.

The chase wasn't over yet.

CHAPTER 31 - INTO THE FIRE

As soon as they made it to Deception Pass and unloaded, an explosion sent a shockwave through the trees, shaking loose a shower of pine needles and debris. Graham threw himself down, shielding Lawoaka and her baby as the fiery glow from the detonation lit up the night. The women huddled together, some crying out in fear, others stunned into silence. The air was thick with smoke, the acrid stench of burning fuel mixing with the damp earth.

Graham's ears rang as he pushed himself up, scanning the shore. The boats that had carried the men were now barely visible through the smoke and fire, their hulls half-shrouded in mist. The flickering flames cast eerie shadows against the trees, distorting the figures that moved through the chaos.

"Arlen!" Graham turned, searching for his friend.

"I got 'em moving!" Arlen called from the tree line, motioning for the survivors to get farther inland. His face was streaked with dirt and sweat, his breath coming hard. "But we don't have much time!"

They didn't. The explosion had bought them a moment, but it wouldn't be enough.

Footsteps pounded through the undergrowth. Shouts in Arabic carried through the night, voices thick with urgency and command.

They were coming.

Graham wiped rain from his face and gritted his teeth. He had to draw them away. If the enemy found the women, it would be over.

He grabbed Arlen's shoulder. "Get them to the road. If we don't make it—"

"Shut up." Arlen shoved him away. "You're making it."

Graham didn't have time to argue. He grabbed both rifles, one in each hand, and took off toward the burning wreckage. If they wanted him, he'd give them a hell of a chase.

The first shot rang out, splintering a nearby tree trunk. Graham dropped low, rolling behind a fallen log as bullets chewed through the bark overhead. The air crackled with gunfire, the sounds ricocheting off the water and trees, making it impossible to pinpoint how many were after him.

They had snipers.

Damn it.

He adjusted his grip on Arlen's rifle, taking a slow breath. Make every shot count.

A flicker of movement caught his eye through the trees.

Graham squeezed the trigger.

The man went down, collapsing into the wet underbrush with a sharp cry. But another took his place.

More figures moved along the tree line, closing in, their silhouettes shifting in the firelight. The heat from the explosion was still radiating off the sand, steam rising where rain met embers. The mist mixed with the smoke, creating a ghostly battlefield.

He fired again. Another went down.

But then—

Click.

His rifle jammed.

"Shit."

Graham barely had time to react before something crashed through the trees beside him. A figure lunged, tackling him to the ground. They hit hard, rolling in the mud, hands grappling for control.

The man snarled in Arabic, trying to bring a knife down into Graham's ribs.

Graham twisted, wrenching the blade from the man's grip and slamming the butt of his rifle into his attacker's face. The man went limp.

No time to breathe. More were coming.

Where the hell was Corey and the others?

Then, a new sound cut through the chaos.

A horn.

Blinding headlights swept over the trees.

Sam.

The truck skidded to a stop, sending a wave of mud

spraying into the enemy's ranks. Sam leaned out of the driver's window, rifle raised.

"Get in!"

Graham didn't hesitate. He sprinted toward the truck, Arlen and Corey appearing from the darkness beside him gathering the freed prisoners and pushing them into the truck. They barely made it when Sam gunned the engine, tires kicking up dirt as they sped away.

Bullets pinged off the metal frame, sparks flying as the enemy fired after them. The truck jolted over the uneven ground, throwing Graham and Arlen against the side panels as they clung to whatever they could. The wind roared past them, carrying the scent of fire, sweat, and blood.

As they tore away from the ambush site, Graham looked back at the flames licking at the shore. The figures in the distance were shrinking, but they weren't giving up. He could see them regrouping, already planning their next move.

Sam shouted over the roar of the engine. "They're not done yet!"

Graham nodded grimly, pressing a hand to his ribs. The bruises from the fight were already setting in, but pain was the least of his worries.

They had escaped.

For now.

CHAPTER 32 - THE ESCAPE FROM DECEPTION PASS

The truck barreled down the rain-slicked road, tires skidding slightly as Sam fought to keep control. The engine whined, struggling under the weight of its passengers and the added pressure of their desperate escape. Gunfire rattled behind them, stray rounds pinging off the truck bed, but they had no choice but to keep going.

Graham clutched his rifle, scanning the road ahead while Corey leaned out the window, firing back at the enemy vehicles giving chase. The muzzle flashes illuminated his grim expression, rain dripping from his chin as he squeezed off another round. In the back, Arlen braced a wounded prisoner, pressing down on a makeshift bandage to slow the bleeding. The woman groaned, his breath shallow, but Arlen didn't stop. His hands were slick with blood, his jaw set in determination.

"We're taking too much fire! I need more ammo." Corey shouted over the roar of the engine.

Sam gritted his teeth. "In the case behind you. Hold on!"

A bullet struck the side mirror, shattering it. Glass sprayed across Sam's arm as he jerked the wheel to the right, narrowly avoiding a patch of broken asphalt. The truck fishtailed but kept going, mud kicking up in its wake. A quick glance at the gauges told him something was wrong—the temperature gauge was spiking, the engine coughing as if protesting the abuse.

Graham saw it too. "We've got a problem."

"Yeah," Sam muttered. "I see it. We're not making it back like this."

The realization settled over the group like a lead weight. They were still miles from Graham's camp, and the truck wasn't going to last that long under this kind of punishment.

Then, headlights appeared ahead of them, coming fast from the opposite direction.

"Shit," Corey breathed, reloading his rifle. "More hostiles?"

Sam's grip tightened on the wheel, ready to force them off the road if needed. But as the truck came into clearer view, Graham caught sight of the driver—Bang.

"It's Bang!" Graham shouted. Relief flooded his voice.

"Thank God," Sam muttered. "Hold on—we're switching rides."

Sam veered to the side, aiming for a stretch of broken pavement just wide enough to give them cover. The truck sputtered and coughed, its death rattle growing louder.

Smoke curled from under the hood. It wouldn't hold out much longer. As they skidded to a stop, Sam threw it into park. "Everyone out! Now!"

The freed prisoners scrambled out first, their faces pale with exhaustion and fear. Arlen hauled the wounded woman over his shoulder while Corey kept his rifle trained on the road behind them. Graham helped a woman with an injured leg out of the truck, his heart pounding against his ribs.

"Leave it!" Sam ordered. "We block the road with it."

Corey slammed the door shut and gave it a hard shove, letting the truck roll just enough to become an obstacle. It wouldn't stop the chase vehicles permanently, but it would slow them down.

Bang's truck roared up beside them, the headlights cutting through the rain. The doors flung open before the vehicle had even come to a full stop. "Move! Move! Move!" Bang shouted.

Graham was the last to climb into the back, pulling himself up as Bang floored the accelerator. The tires kicked up mud and gravel as they sped off, leaving the disabled truck and their pursuers behind. Just as they cleared the bend, a gunshot rang out, and something exploded behind them—their abandoned truck.

The force of the explosion rattled the chassis of Bang's truck, the heat momentarily cutting through the rain-chilled air. The fiery glow illuminated the road behind them, black smoke curling into the sky. The enemy was still coming.

"They're still after us!" Corey shouted, his knuckles white as he gripped his rifle.

Bang didn't ease up on the gas. "They won't keep up. Not if we make it to the pass."

Graham wiped rain from his face, glancing back at the wreckage they left behind. The fight wasn't over. Not yet.

But at least, for now, they had a head start.

CHAPTER 33 - THE LAST CALL

The sound of the wind and rain hammered against the metal cab. Graham held on to the frame as Bang pushed the vehicle as fast as it would go, his hands tight on the wheel, his face a mask of focus. The freed prisoners huddled together in the back, exhausted, but wide-eyed with fear. Corey, next to Graham, kept his rifle propped on the side, scanning the road behind them. The sound of an engine in the distance made him curse under his breath.

"They're still coming."

Bang didn't flinch. "Dad, we can't lead them back to camp."

Graham already knew it. If they brought the enemy straight to their front door, there would be no stopping the massacre that followed. The camp wasn't ready for this. They had too many wounded, too many mouths to feed, too many people who had spent too much time just trying to survive. And yet, they always knew this moment might come. He grabbed the radio from the dash and switched to their frequency.

"Macy, get Clarisse. Right now."

There was static for a moment before Macy's voice broke through. "She's here."

Graham closed his eyes briefly, relief washing through him. He and Clarisse had been through too much together to waste time on panic.

When she spoke, her voice was steady. "Tell me."

"We can't lead them back," he said, his voice just as calm. "It's time."

There was silence. But only for a second.

"I'll start moving them now," Clarisse said. That was it. No arguing. No hesitation. Just action.

Graham looked at Sam, who had been listening. He exhaled, gripping his rifle tighter. "Where?"

Graham didn't answer at first. Instead, he kept his eyes on the dark road ahead. "You know. Codeword: Ashfall."

Sam sucked in a breath. He knew what that meant. The three of them did. Those that were a part of this from the beginning. The plan had been in place for years. It had always been a last resort, a fallback in case the camp ever became too compromised. They had never wanted to use it. Dalton had warned them it was a last resort. But now, they had no choice. And in his heart, he knew Rick and Dalton would both agree, it was time.

Clarisse was already barking orders in the background, her voice carrying through the radio. "Macy, get Paige and Mark. Start loading vehicles. McCann, get everyone armed and prepped to move. Sam's already with you—"

"Yes," Graham cut in. "Sam's here. He's with us."

There was a brief pause. Then, Clarisse shifted gears without missing a beat. "All right. I'll need you to keep a perimeter while we pack. We leave in fifteen minutes." That wasn't a lot of time. But it was all they had.

The truck jerked as Bang took a sharp turn, the tires barely gripping the wet road. "We're losing them," Bang grunted. "But not for long."

Graham pressed the radio against his lips. "Make sure they all know. Leave nothing behind. We can't come back."

"I know." Clarisse's voice softened, just a fraction. "See you there." The radio cut off.

For a few seconds, the only sound in the truck was the rumble of the engine and the measured breath of those who had just lost everything. Graham let the weight of the decision settle in his chest. They had just abandoned the place they'd fought to protect for so long.

Bang's voice cut through the tension.

"Where is Ashfall?" he asked, sparing a glance in the rearview mirror.

Graham didn't answer immediately. He could feel the others watching him, waiting. He shifted slightly, staring out the rain-streaked windshield at the road stretching endlessly before them.

"Ashfall is the end of the road," he said finally. "And the beginning of something else. A place they will never follow."

Bang grunted, turning his attention back to driving. "As long as it keeps my family safe."

Graham didn't answer. Because truthfully, he didn't know.

CHAPTER 34 - THE BREAKING POINT

Clarisse stood in the center of the camp, her breath tight in her chest as she took in the stunned faces around her. People weren't moving fast enough. They weren't moving *at all*. The rain had finally stopped, but a chill clung to the air. The night was eerily still, as if the forest around them was holding its breath, waiting for the worst.

They *had* to go. *Now.*

She stepped forward, voice sharp. "MOVE! I don't care what you're holding onto—drop it and get to your assigned vehicles. We leave in *ten minutes.*"

No one moved.

Clarisse clenched her jaw and turned to McCann, who was standing like a statue near the firepit. "Get them moving, McCann! If they're not packed and loaded in five, leave them behind."

That did it. A ripple of urgency spread through the crowd. People scrambled, grabbing whatever meager possessions they had left. There was no time for sentimentality.

Across the camp, Macy rushed toward the storage tent, grabbing emergency supplies. Mark and Paige were securing weapons. The sound of hurried, hushed conversations layered over the rustling of bags, the slamming of truck doors, the shifting of boots on damp earth.

Clarisse turned her attention to the girl they had just taken in—Leila. The girl stood near the firepit, her arms wrapped tightly around herself. She was barely upright. Her eyes were wild, darting between the people moving around her and the darkened tree line beyond.

She *knew* what was coming.

Leila took a step back, her hands trembling. "They're coming," she whispered, her voice barely audible over the clamor of the camp. "They're coming. They're going to find us."

Clarisse grabbed her by the shoulders. "Then we need to be *gone* before they do. You want to survive? Get in a truck. *Now.*"

The girl shook her head frantically. "You don't understand! You don't know what they do to people who run."

Clarisse's stomach clenched, but she didn't let it show. She softened her grip, lowering her voice. "We *do* know, Leila. That's why we're leaving. But if you freeze up now, you *will* get caught. And they won't stop at just you."

Leila swallowed hard, her breath coming in ragged gasps. Then, finally, she gave a small, terrified nod.

Clarisse turned to Macy. "Get her in Mark's truck. Don't let her out of your sight."

Macy pulled Leila along, murmuring reassurances as they disappeared into the throng of people preparing to leave.

Clarisse exhaled, rubbing a hand over her face.

Then she saw Paige, standing off to the side, hesitating.

Clarisse marched over to her, anger surging hot in her veins. "Paige, what the *hell* are you doing? Get Cheryl and get to your truck."

Paige met her gaze, her lips pressed into a thin line. "I—I don't know if I should go."

Clarisse stiffened. "What?"

Paige put her hands on her hips, shaking her head. "Graham's always had a plan, but this? We don't even know what will happen there. What if I take my unborn child into something worse? What if—"

Clarisse cut her off, stepping closer, her voice low and cold. "If you run now, with his child, he'll never forgive you. He'll *never* stop looking. He won't just let it go, Paige. He'll hunt you down."

Paige flinched, her gaze dropping to the dirt.

Clarisse pressed on. "You know I'm right. Graham is a lot of things but *letting go* isn't one of them."

Paige exhaled, shaking her head. "I just... I don't know if I can do this. I know where Ashfall is. Graham told me long ago."

Clarisse's voice softened, but it didn't lose its edge. "Then you know our position is that compromised. It has advantages as well as its risks. We have preventive measures in place. Paige, don't do it for you. Do it for your child."

A long silence stretched between them. Then, finally, Paige nodded. Just once.

Clarisse didn't waste another second. "Good. Now get moving."

Paige turned and hurried toward the convoy. Clarisse exhaled sharply and turned back to the camp.

They had *minutes* left.

She walked toward the nearest truck and stepped up high so they could all see her. "FINAL CALL! We leave *now* or we *don't leave at all!*"

The last stragglers scrambled to their places. Clarisse jumped down, her gut twisting as she scanned the camp one last time to make sure she spotted her own children in McCann's vehicle.

Goodbye, home.

She climbed into her truck, slamming the door shut just as the first set of headlights cut through the trees.

They were out of time.

CHAPTER 35 - A NEW HORIZON

The sun was blinding.

Graham stepped out of the truck, squinting against the relentless glare, his breath already sticking to the back of his throat. The heat wrapped around him like a suffocating blanket, pressing down on his shoulders, leeching every ounce of moisture from the air. The earth beneath his boots was cracked, parched, the color of old bones. Dust stirred as he shifted his weight, carried away by the faintest breeze, a ghost of movement in an otherwise lifeless wasteland.

The contrast to the world they had left behind was staggering. There were no towering trees here, no dense canopies of green swaying in the wind, no scent of rain-soaked earth. Instead, the air tasted of rust and something chemical—something wrong. The land stretched out before them, barren and hollow, a place stripped of life long before their arrival.

A row of buildings loomed in the distance, skeletal remains of a forgotten past. Most were little more than crumbling walls and gaping doorways, their windows shattered, jagged edges glinting in the sunlight like broken teeth. A faded **KEEP OUT** sign flapped weakly on a bent metal post nearby, its edges curling, the red warning letters nearly erased by time.

One by one, the others climbed down from the truck, shielding their eyes, adjusting their packs, taking in the nothingness that stretched ahead. Gone were the towering trees, the sound of the wind sifting through branches, the comfort of misted mornings. Here, the sky pressed down on them, the land open and exposed.

They had reached the place no one had ever wanted to come to.

Clarisse moved with quiet efficiency, unloading a heavy-duty military case from the truck's bed. She cracked it open, revealing rows of small black devices with frayed yellow labels.

Graham watched as she picked one up and tested the screen. The others stood still, waiting. Even the wind had died here, as if the land itself was holding its breath.

She looped the first detector around Addy's neck, then another over her son's, adjusting them carefully. The weight of it—of what it meant—settled over them all. A silent, invisible threat wrapped itself around them, a reminder that safety was a concept long left behind.

No one asked where they were.

Because everyone already knew.

Clarisse moved down the line, looping another over Paige's head. Paige glanced at it, grimacing. "And if it starts beeping?"

Clarisse didn't sugarcoat it. "You leave. Fast."

Paige swallowed. "Great. Fantastic." Then she muttered, "Well, it's not my fault when the baby comes out with four ears."

A few tired chuckles spread through the group, but it didn't last. Laughter was too fragile here, too easily swallowed by the weight of reality.

Graham scanned their faces—faces that had been through war, starvation, near death—and yet, this… this was what made them hesitate.

This wasn't a battle. This was a kind of surrender.

His eyes met Clarisse's as she handed him his own detector. Neither of them had to say it. They had known this moment would come, had planned for it, dreaded it, avoided it… but here they were.

Tehya stood near the back, her arms crossed, gaze locked on the horizon as Scout leaned against her. She wasn't arguing, wasn't questioning. Just staring ahead. Graham didn't know what she was thinking, but it was there—her mother's quiet strength, the way she processed things without speaking.

Clarisse finished distributing the devices. The former prisoners adjusted the cords around their necks, shifting uneasily, as if they could feel the weight of the past pressing on them, tethering them to whatever history lingered in this place.

Graham took one last look at their surroundings. The

buildings in the distance, long abandoned, filled with ghosts of another time.

There was no going back.

They weren't sure what lay ahead.

But it didn't matter.

This was the last chance they had.

As the others began to move through the gated area into the abandoned space beyond, Graham hesitated. Something was half-buried near the gate, rusted and broken, half-hidden beneath the dust and time.

He crouched, running a gloved hand over the twisted metal. The dirt came away in streaks, revealing the faded black lettering beneath.

The name was unmistakable.

HANFORD.

His fingers clenched. His breath stalled.

The others had already gone ahead, disappearing into the empty shell of what once had been.

But this place… they had known of it long before they arrived.

Dalton had warned them. Rick, too, in the days before he was gone. There had always been whispers, rumors of what had been left behind here—of a weapon no one had ever wanted to see used. A weapon buried beneath time, beneath regret.

Graham swallowed hard.

They had been forced into this. Forced into taking measures they had sworn never to take.

Let's hope it didn't come to that.

He straightened, inhaled the thick, chemical-tinged air, and followed the others through the gate.

Because if the past was waiting for them here, there was no turning back now.

ABOUT THE AUTHOR

A.R. Shaw is a bestselling author of post-apocalyptic and survival thrillers, weaving gripping tales of resilience, hope, and the human spirit. With a background in crafting immersive worlds, she has captivated readers with stories that explore survival in the face of adversity. When she's not writing, she enjoys seeking out inspiration in the quiet moments of life. Discover more of her work at **ARShawBooks.com**.

ALSO BY A. R. SHAW

Survival isn't just a story—it's a way of life.

Discover over **50 gripping post-apocalyptic and survival thrillers** by A.R. Shaw.

Explore them all at **ARShawBooks.com**

Made in United States
Troutdale, OR
04/14/2025